Mastering Martial Arts

A Complete Guide To TAI CHI

WALTER LORINI

Enslow Publishing
101 W. 23rd Street
Suite 240
New York, NY 10011
USA
enslow.com

Published in 2018 by Enslow Publishing, LLC.
101 W. 23rd Street, Suite 240, New York, NY 10011

Library of Congress Cataloging-in-Publication Data

Names: Lorini, Walter, author.
Title: A complete guide to tai chi / Walter Lorini.
Description: New York, NY : Enslow Publishing, 2018. | Series: Mastering martial arts | Includes bibliographical references and index. | Audience: Grades 6-12.
Identifiers: LCCN 2017005211 | ISBN 9780766085374 (library bound)
Subjects: LCSH: Tai chi.
Classification: LCC GV504 .L65 2018 | DDC 613.7/148—dc23
LC record available at https://lccn.loc.gov/2017005211

Printed in the United States of America

To Our Readers: We have done our best to make sure all websites in this book were active and appropriate when we went to press. However, the author and the publisher have no control over and assume no liability for the material available on those websites or on any websites they may link to. Any comments or suggestions can be sent by e-mail to customerservice@enslow.com.

Contents

Introduction

In this tai chi (or *tai chi chuan*) manual, you'll discover a fascinating martial arts discipline. Having recently arrived in the Western world, tai chi's popularity is consistently growing, with no signs of stopping. We're illustrating this discipline here to show how the consistent and conscious practice of tai chi has the ability to improve one's quality of life. To fully comprehend the reasons why this series of techniques, created around 1000 BCE, is still practiced and studied, one must first analyze the diverse aspects characterizing it: its history, basic theory, the benefits it brings to those who practice it, and, finally, its correct execution.

Tai chi can present itself as a sequence of simple and fluid movements, almost a dance that awakens the curiosity. In China during early mornings, one can see many people practicing very slow movements in the park, hardly seeming to move. For example, some practitioners may remain completely still in front of a plant for many minutes, almost as if to embrace it, overwhelmed by a mysterious sensation. These acts are rather far from the Western mentality and concept of sport or exercise.

"Tai chi chuan" literally means "supreme ultimate boxing." It is a defensive exercise and therapeutic technique to improve one's health and combines the Chinese Taoist theories of yin and yang and the five elements. Tai chi employs the use of slow movements that are designed to circulate *chi* (energy or inner breath) by using inner muscle stretching techniques. These moves are smooth and give life to a complete system of both mental and physical exercise. In tai chi, all of the qualities the Western world is not accustomed to using are applied, such as movement with intercostal muscles, breathing with the diaphragmatic muscle, and using the power of tendons and bones. Tai chi can thus improve one's body physically and make it more flexible and responsive. As the body ages, it becomes more rigid, and ailments like joint aches arise, which can greatly decrease one's quality of life. In our hectic everyday lives, we are often too busy to think about our health. When problems like these appear, we resort to alleviating them hastily with chemical medications.

Pills are by no means the only possible remedy for aches and pains: it has been shown that for many diseases, it is sometimes sufficient to use the mind, combined with the use of energy and the body, to obtain the same benefits provided by medication.

Thanks to continued practice, many Chinese scholars have understood that the combination of the body and mind can be effectively used to defend against diseases as well as an opponent in combat. A healthy and trained body can, without a doubt, overcome many problems, both internal and external. The tai chi student's ultimate goals are learning the

The ancient practice of tai chi attracts many practitioners.

art of self-defense, strengthening balance, and improving health. But only consistent practice can truly change the way one's body feels. Tai chi is one of the best and safest ways to reach the consciousness of one's own abilities, provided that training is not rushed and that the student doesn't give up at the first moment of difficulty. It only takes one tai chi session to understand why this book was written and why enthusiasts continue to practice and spread this discipline.

History, Techniques, and Theory

History

Cataloging the full history of tai chi would be a very long and intense undertaking. In this short overview, we must limit our discussion and consideration of tai chi to the four crucial periods of time that are most representative of its development:

1. Before the Chen Village or the Wudang Mountains
2. the Chen Village period
3. the period of diffusion from the Chen Village
4. the period from the birth of the People's Republic until now

As we consider the history of tai chi, it is important to note that, as a global sport, it has experienced many evolutions both within and outside its country of origin. In this chapter, we will frame our discussion around tai chi's origins, its development in China, and its fundamental techniques.

Wu chi, "tai chi is born from wu chi."

The Origin of Tai Chi Before the Chen Village or Wudang Mountains (5000 BCE–1644 CE)

The birth of tai chi goes back to the Taoist doctrines referring to diet and nutrition. These practices incorporated movements of expansion and extension, combined with breathing techniques, to increase and improve the circulation of chi in the body. The *chi kung* techniques, like doctor Hua To's exercise of the five animals, were famous during the Liang dynasty (502–557 CE). These techniques are considered precursors of tai chi, as they displayed the emerging principles of the discipline. At this point, tai chi was not yet identified with its name, which would only come to appear in later historical documents.

Many historians have traced the birth of tai chi to Zhang Sanfeng, a Taoist monk who, according to legend, lived from 1247 to 1460 during the Northern Song (960–1279), Yuan (1279–1368), and beginning of the Ming (1368–1644) dynasties. According to two accounts, the legend states that the hermit developed his art after a sudden moment of intuition. The first chronicle describes how Zhang observed a fight between a crane and a snake. Meditating on what he had seen, he invented tai chi, which combines the agile movements of the crane with the smooth, flexible actions of the snake.

The other version states that it was the mythical Black Emperor who suggested the combat method to Zhang during a dream. Perhaps, as historian Li Yang Ang suggests, Zhang simply modified some Shaolin techniques that he considered too rigid with Taoist concepts of internal alchemy he learned in the Wudang Mountains.

It is said that Zhang Sanfeng lived for more than 200 years, and that in 1459 he was bestowed with immortality by Emperor Zhengtong, the seventh Ming emperor.

Another legend traces the birth of tai chi to Wang Zong Yue, who was the first to call the art by its present name. His ideas were based on the Taoist theory of yin and yang, but it is almost certain that his contribution to the emerging discipline was limited to the writing of a systematic compendium of the principles of tai chi, which led many to think he was the effective founder of the discipline. Perhaps it was one of his students who took this knowledge to Chen Village.

The Chen Village Period (1644–1680)

For many historians, the birth of tai chi dates back to a more recent time—that of General Chen Wang Ting (1600–1680), a martial arts expert who united his military experience with the existing knowledge of two important books of the era: *The Thirty-Two Classic Martial Positions* and *The Yellow Court Classic*.

In the topics Ting discusses, the name "tai chi" is not mentioned, which indicates that it either had not yet been created or that it was not yet known by name. *Shaolin tong bei* was the preferred school of martial arts in Chen Village before Ting Wang Ting. When Chen returned from the war in 1644, he began to teach a new type of exercises to the members of his family and the city, modifying the Shaolin style and introducing the Taoist concepts of yin and yang. This new style quickly changed into a popular form of combat. Ting had codified five variations of the style, but by the time of Chen Chang Xing (1771–1853), the style typologies had already multiplied. Xing was called the straight man because of his ability to maintain balance while he performed techniques. According to legends, he could make an attacker fly across the room without even leaving his seat.

After the fourteenth generation of the Chen family, several Chen style branches were produced. These branches included the Chen You Ben and Chen Qing Ping styles. Along with *xiaojia* (small frame), these new variations helped modernize the existing Chen style, making it less martial in nature.

The Period of Diffusion from Chen Village (1800–1949)

After the first divisions within the Chen family, it didn't take much time for the members of the other families to appropriate the secrets of tai chi and add their own modifications.

Perhaps most famously, Yang Lu Chan (1799–1872) is known for

Zhang Sanfeng, the immortal.

setting the wheels in motion for the development of the Yang style, which draws inspiration from the Chen style. Yang worked in Beijing, in a pharmacy governed by the people of Chen Village. One day, a monk came and begged for food. Not satisfied with what he received, the monk became angry, grabbed a large stone, and blocked the door of the store.

The proprietor of the store defeated the monk quickly, with agile movements. Suddenly curious, Yang asked the owner what form of combat he practiced. The man replied that he practiced tai chi, one of the popular martial arts taught in his hometown, and though he was not an expert, he had still defeated the monk. The proprietor presented Yang to Chen Chang Xing, but Xing only taught him the sequence of the forms without revealing their true contents.

After three years of exercise, Yang lost a fight and decided to return to the village, where he studied to improve. Xing, already old, considered Yang's commitment and decided to teach him the secrets of the art. Shortly after, Yang challenged a monk and killed him. In an attempt to escape justice, Yang sought refuge in Beijing, and as a result of his time there, the Yang style began to make its way into the imperial court.

Yang Lu Chan had a student named Wu Yu Xiang (1812–1880), who went to seek out Yang's teacher Chen Chang Xing. Because Chen Chang Xing was too old to teach him, Wu traveled to a neighboring village in order to learn from another Chen style expert, a teacher named Chen Qing Ping (1795-1868). With Wu Yu Xiang, a new branch of tai chi was born, the Wu style, also called the Hao style because it was popularized by his disciple Hao Wei Zhen (1849–1920). Yang Lu Chan's second son, Yang Ban Hou, had a student called Wu Jian Quan (1870–1942), who codified the Wu style.

Another famous master of the Chen style of the seventeenth generation was Chen Fa Ke (1887–1957), who had two sons. The first son, Chen Zhao Kui (1928–1981), was active in Shanghai until 1966 and instructed masters like He Bing Quan, Ma Hong, and Chen Zhao Xu, the father of Chen Xiao Wang. The other son of Yang Lu Chan, Yan Jian Hou (1839–1917), had three sons of his own, among whom were Yang Chao Hsing and Chao Chin (1883–1936), who was also called Chen Fu. Chen Fu is perhaps one of the most famous masters. Despite the fact that he began practicing tai chi late in his life, he is responsible for developing a majority of the 108 postures that make up the Yang style.

Currently, the most famous representatives of the two styles are Chen Xiao Wang for the Chen style and Yang Zhen Duo for the Yang style. It is interesting to note that the current effective development of these styles throughout the world is due in large part to students with no relation to these families, like Cheng Man Ching (1901–1975), a writer who translated and popularized the classic tai chi books in the United States and Taiwan; Fu Zhong Wen, whose son-in-law taught in Shanghai until his death; and George Xu, Yang Jwing Ming, Liang Shou Yu, and Jou Tsung Hwa, who all have brought their knowledge to the West. There are also an infinite number of local Chinese and Western masters currently teaching around the world.

The Period from the Birth of the People's Republic Until Now

In later years, as China began to build relationships with other countries, tai chi experienced a major move to the West. The ancient techniques are used to maintain the health of millions of people at little cost by focusing on aspects related more closely to health rather than the discipline's military elements. At universities and in many sports clubs, there are trained coaches exercising in parks.

The direct descendants of the different styles have continued teaching in China and abroad, while the Chinese government systematically hid all knowledge of the past until the death of Mao Zedong. Since then, many things have changed in China, including a new recognition of tai chi techniques represented by the families of ancient traditions like Chen and Yang.

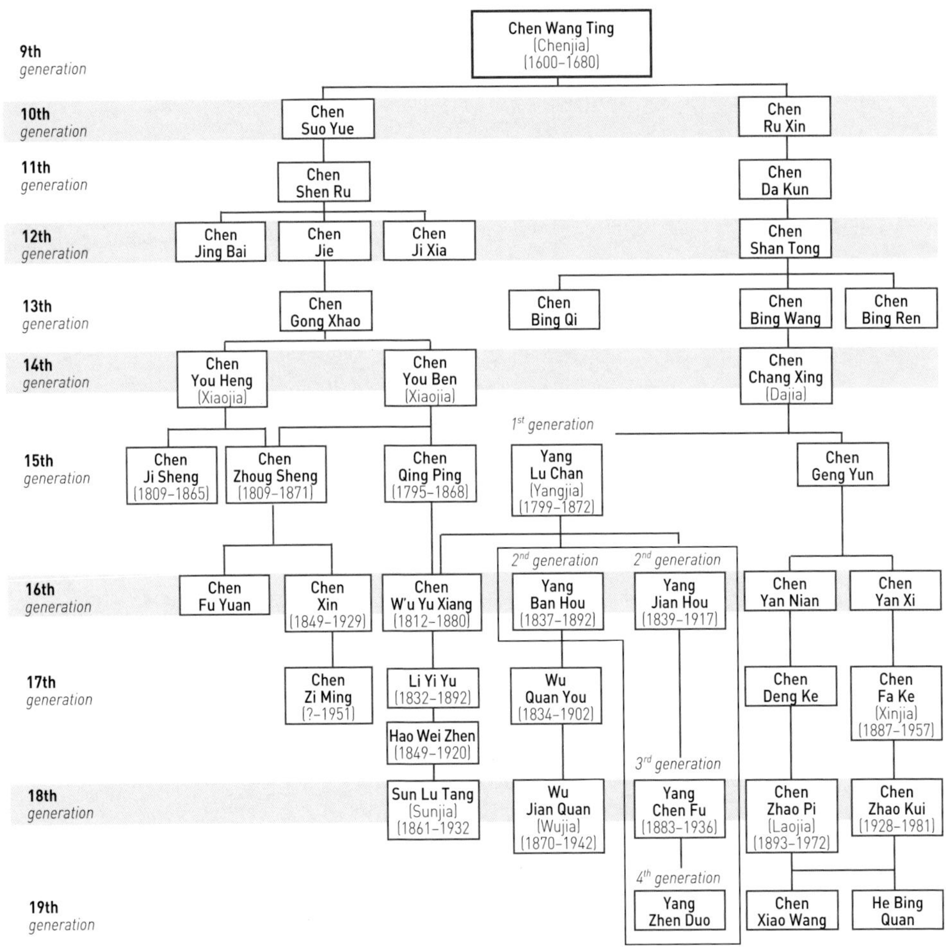

This is the genealogical tree of tai chi chuan from its birth in Chen Village to our days. The Yang family started its own genealogy with Yang Lu Chan.

How to Distinguish the Different Tai Chi Styles

At the beginning of the 1970s, the only tai chi that was known in the West was the Yang style, a slow movement that the first students considered more gymnastics than martial art.

However, in 1985, cultural and political shifts in China allowed for more transparency with the West. Practitioners of tai chi who lived outside of China discovered that the Yang style was only one of the five *neijia* styles of tai chi still taught and practiced in China. Furthermore, the existence of the Wudang style was also discovered, a style even older than Chen. In this section, the essential differences between the five styles are illustrated, as well as the Wudang and modern styles, emphasizing their characteristics.

The Chen Style

The Chen style is actually divided into two styles: the old, *laojia* (first structure), codified by Chen Zhao Pi (1893–1972), and the new, *xinjia*, from Chen Fa Ke (1887–1957). Originally, it was composed of five forms, but it is now reduced to two principles: *diyuli*, which constitutes the basis of the thirteen fundamental techniques, and *pauchui*, also known as the Cannon Fist. In the latter style, the movements follow largely stretched spirals, and the positions are exaggerated; in some movements there are jumps that are eliminated from other types of tai chi. The principle characteristics can be summarized by the following:

- Continuous change of position
- Finalized with a strike once the technique is finished
- The body is seen as a sphere
- The body is "opened" and "closed" alternately

These characteristics allow the style to be well suited for younger students and to all those who are interested in the military aspect of tai chi.

The Yang Style

This is the style of tai chi that is most well known around the world. Because of its continuous, slow movements, it is well suited for everyone, young and old, and relatively easy to learn. The Yang style is a derivative of the

Chen style

Chen style that was simplified and modified in order to make it more accessible to the imperial court and then to the general public. It is practiced in the eighty movements created by Yang Chen Fu (1883–1936), but it is well disseminated in the Twenty-Four Movements form (also called the Beijing form), and in the form of thirty-seven movements (which comes from the Cheng Man Ching school). Teachers of the Yang style use smooth movements to guide those who use tai chi in searching for concentration and relaxation. In fact, it is also practiced as moving meditation, from which is where it derives its great popularity. The principle characteristics are:

- Great stability in the movements
- Continuity, as if the movements were waves

Yang style

- Smooth nature of the techniques
- Flowing changes like the majestic flight of the eagle

The Wu Style

The principle of this style is derived from the Yang style, known as *zhongjia* (middle structure), from which it took its natural characteristic movements. It is continuous and relaxed. To distinguish it from the Yang style, founder Wu Jian Quan (1870–1942) introduced turns and twists of the torso, which are done with the spine in a straight, vertical line. The body, during the execution of this style, inclines slightly forward. It is the most popular form of tai chi after the Yang and Chen styles and suited for all those searching for movements with strong stretching components. Its main characteristics are:

- Central balance in every position
- Superior concentration using will
- Settlement on the ground
- Sensibility in continuous change

The Wu or Hao Style

This little-known style is derived from the Chen style, xiaojia, popularized by Chen Qing Ping (1795–1868). It is characterized by narrow movements done standing almost completely upright. It is a fundamental search for the circulation of internal chi, mainly using low positions or twisting movements. It places a lot of importance on the concepts of full and empty.

Despite its apparent simplicity, it is one of the most difficult styles to practice, and so it is not very popular outside of China. However, it is widespread in Beijing, Shanghai, and Nanking, where it's practiced by the traditional tai chi students.

The Sun Style

The last of the five tai chi styles has taken the essence of the *bagua* as its principle technique, since its founder, Sun Lu Tang (1861–1932), was one of the greatest masters of the style. He studied with Hao Wei Zhen (1849–1920), a successor of the style of the Wu family. From this union emerged a style of continuous movements forward and backward, inspired by the techniques of the Yang,

Chen, and Wu families.
The movements are rigid but sometimes twisting. This is a style suited for those who are already familiar with the other styles and want to further their knowledge.

The Wudang Tai Chi

In recent years, there has been interest in a tai chi style derived directly from the Wudang Mountains, homeland to many Taoist philosophers. This has led to the development of a tai chi style that combines the idea of yin and yang with the movements of two internal styles (*xingyi* and bagua). This style reflects various techniques practiced and developed by Taoist monks.

It is inspired by the the large combat between a crane and a snake, which founder Zhang Sanfeng had studied in the Wudang Mountains. This style is identified for the most part by the large variety of characterized movements, with positions that are sometimes high and sometimes low, depending on whether the moving part is the crane or the snake.

Sun style

Wu or Hao style

Modern Tai Chi

The use of competitive tai chi has come out of these styles, which have been codified by the Chinese National Research Institute of Wushu (that is, kung fu). A simplified version was created to promote a universal tai chi practice. To unify the rules of the different schools of tai chi, especially for international competition, forty-two tai chi movements have been codified that assume positions from all of the styles mentioned. As a general rule, we should always bear in mind this diversity that was generated by the changes produced during the numerous centuries of tai chi's existence.

This book delves only into the form called the Twenty-Four Movements, but the theoretical concepts presented are also valid for students of all the other styles.

The Fundamentals According to the Theory of Yin and Yang

To understand the theoretical base of tai chi, we need to learn about the basic philosophical ideas of Taoism, the cultural heritage of the Chinese that rationally explains how this movement was born. The Chinese think of the universe as a series of interconnected organisms rather than a connection of separate entities. Every part of the universe is connected with every other part, and to exist, each object needs its opposite, like day needs night, man needs woman, and north needs south.

This duality also exists within our bodies, as the Chinese proverb says: "You cannot understand your body if you do not understand the universe that surrounds you." The human being is a body between heaven and earth and is influenced by both.

The traditional symbol of yin and yang.

This concept has been represented as a circle, divided by two drops, one white (yang), and one black (yin), affirming the unity within duality. Inside the two divisions of yin and yang, there is a point of the complementary color to demonstrate that nothing is absolute or pure. For example, when a solar eclipse occurs during the day, or a lunar eclipse at night, we accept this duality as a normal part of life.

The symbol turns within itself, because the parts are always in motion, in permanent transformation. The drawing of the figure lacks the profound depth of a sphere within space. Tai chi is based on this theory, and every student should search for the duality in every position, uniting the yin and the yang without interruption, with the breath (inhaling and exhaling) maintaining a uniform rhythm.

If one tries to begin with a determined rhythm of breath, one should maintain this until the end, without variations; this allows one to perform balanced movements. On the other hand, a faulty and discontinuous rhythm, even if well executed, can prove to be useless or even harmful.

Yin and yang are interdependent: in any position, the front leg is considered yang, and the back leg is considered yin. Similarly, the front part of the body is always yin, and the back always yang. When this duality between the different positions is understood, it is necessary to know that the terms "yin" and "yang" should not be understood as absolute, but more like relatives. In fact, there are further subdivisions within the interior of yin and yang. While this can seem complicated for those studying the theory of tai chi, it is important to search for the essence of the movements, because profound knowledge of the discipline comes from constant, daily practice.

Because yin and yang are represented as drops—small at first, but always growing larger—the succession of opposites never occurs quickly, but instead gradually: one part increases while the other decreases. For example, during the day, the sun rises from the horizon (increasing the yang), and the night moves away (diminishing the yin). When, in the evening, the sun begins to descend below the horizon (diminishing the yang), the night approaches (increasing the yin). According to the Chinese, this principle is valid for everything in the universe, living beings or inanimate objects.

While executing the movements, it is important to keep in mind that each yin movement should be accompanied with an increase of yang: one must open oneself outward, emptying inwardly during the yang phase and showing external relaxation during the yin phase.

This theory was born 3,000 years ago during the Zhou dynasty when the famous *Classic of Changes* was written.

This text is divided into two parts: the first contains the *Classic of Changes*, also called the *I Ching*, an oracle or book of probabilities, while the second holds the philosophical and theoretical explanations.

The basic theory of yin and yang is explored in the text as well.

In short, the symbol of yin and yang is composed of several images that are all based on a circular line representing the integrity of the universe: the central curvature of the circle divides the opposites; the two drops symbolize the interdependency of the opposites; the dots of the opposite color in each drop illustrate the nonabsolute vision of the yin and yang.

The Essence of the Techniques

When students execute the tai chi movements, they discover how in every technique one of the eight life-giving forces is hidden within each exercise.

These constitute the essence of the technique, the component that in every position is the most pivotal to its execution and that the student should pay the most attention to in these specific movements.

To achieve the objectives of the tai chi movements—to use the inner force to protect oneself against an attack—it is necessary, according to the classic texts, to understand the forces of the body.

Students can learn how to develop and understand the forces of the body through a two-person exercise called pushing hands. This exercise is often practiced as a warm up in order to prepare the body for movement. In this chapter, we indicate how to properly train these forces, while the practical part of each position indicates which force should be used. The eight forces are:

- *Pengjing* (force of expansion)
- *Lujing* (force of absorption and deviation)
- *Jijing* (force of concentration)
- *Anjing* (force of pushing)
- *Caijing* (force of pulling)
- *Liejing* (force of division)
- *Zhoujing* (elbow force)
- *Kaojing* (shoulder force)

THE PENGJING (Force of Expansion)

This fundamental force is used in many techniques that require expansion and in almost all of the positions that are executed in the expectation of an attack. To train the pengjing, students need to feel as though their insides have expanded like a ball, inflating the whole body from the arms and legs to the fingertips.

From the natural position, one can imagine that the *tan tien* (abdominal region) is expanding, a feeling that continues throughout the body. The final sensation is to be relaxed but still strong and full of energy.

In order to train these forces, repeat the two movements multiple times without interruption.

THE LUJING (Force of Absorption)

The lujing is the force of absorption. After the expansion of pengjing, one must think about deflating oneself, intent on absorbing something with the hands, until all the concentration is on the tan tien (the center of gravity of the standing body), pointing four fingers below the belly button. In this moment, there will be a sensation of absorption, and one will feel that the belly is deflating while the body fills with chi. The hands move from the previous position to the abdomen, with the intention of absorbing this force.

THE JIJING (Force of Concentration)

Every technique of tai chi introduces the possibility of concentrating the entire force of the body to strike areas, even very small ones, reaching the vital points of the opponent.

To train this force, the two hands must be tight and crossed, giving a forceful strike to the shoulder of the person in front of you while you're exhaling. Naturally, all parts of the body can be hit, but normally the partner's back is used so no real harm is caused.

THE ANJING (Force of Pushing)

The force is normally trained by pressing down on the partner's crossed arms with the palms of the hands. Everything is executed during the inhale, bringing in the concentration of the tan tien. It is similar to trying to shut a very full suitcase, placing the palms of the hands on top and pressing down to close it.

THE CAIJING (Force of Pulling)

When you use this force, a ripping motion is performed, like the one that we use to pull a sheet of paper from a notebook without tearing it. This is practiced by tugging the arm slightly in every direction, trying to concentrate all motion into one instant. This is done during the exhalation after concentrating intensely on the tan tien energy itself.

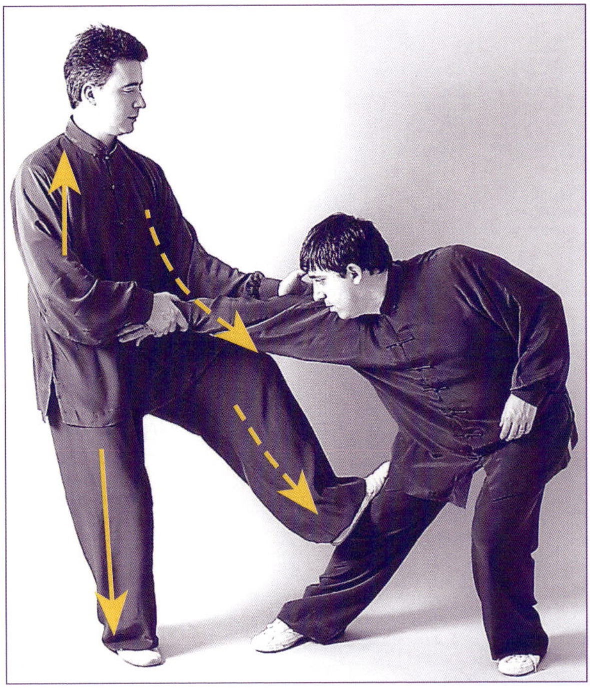

THE LIEJING (Force of Division)

This serves to break your opponent's force, trying to use the whole body to separate one object into two parts. An example of this is trying to tear a sheet of paper in half or break an arm into two parts, using what in Western terms is called a lever. This is trained by separating the hands to the right and left.

THE ZHOUJING (Elbow Force)

This elbow force, often used in the Chen style, concentrates on the possibility of trapping or striking an opponent at a short distance.

It's necessary to rotate and strike to the right and left with the elbows; this helps keep the spine vertical and uses it like a central bolt.

THE KAOJING (Shoulder Force)

This force is used when you are in contact with your opponent's body. It is improperly called shoulder force, but this term should be understood in a more general sense that includes the entire body. This force is used to throw or lift another person.

When this force is controlled (achieved through practice and repetition to understand the hidden energies of the techniques), you can begin to practice.

Instructions for Correct Practice

In this chapter, we illustrate the fundamental points to correctly practice tai chi, beginning with the appropriate body positioning for the movements. The instructions must be respected because, as the Chinese say, "A good plant needs good roots to grow."

Body Preparations

Before beginning to practice tai chi, it's necessary to center oneself and try to get in tune with the new movements.

All of the great masters introduce students to the knowledge of tai chi with respect to the different positions of the body.

At least at the beginning, it's necessary to look at the proper posture in front of the mirror: remember to always keep the head upright, as if hanging from the sky.

When the head is not well aligned, there is a sensation of a lack of balance and vitality. The chin should be tucked in to align the vertebrae.

The gaze should remain concentrated because intention is very important in conscious movement and in achieving precision.

Zhong ding, "being focused."

The tongue should be turned up to decrease the production of saliva. Pronouncing the sound "la," the tip of the tongue comes into contact with the palate. It should remain in this position during the exercises. A mouth that is too tightly closed limits breathing.

The shoulders should be relaxed and symmetrical. The chest does not need to be puffed out but instead held with a slight inward curvature—this helps the breathing and improves the connection between the movement of the torso and the hands. Be sure that the abdomen does not stick out too much and that the legs are well aligned, without bending the knees in.

The stomach is the most important area because it is there that the energy, or *yuanjing* (vital force), resides. Flexing the abdomen stimulates the principle internal organs, like the liver, kidneys, and spleen, which reinforces their functioning.

It's necessary to try to eliminate tension in the spine: imagine being a marionette suspended by a string. It should be as if the string passes through the top of the head to the legs.

The hips and the waist, which connect the lower and upper parts of the body, should be loose, otherwise, energy can't pass to the legs and will create an instability in the body.

The tan tien is situated in the front part of this region, which is where the tai chi movement originates, while the back part, the *ming men* (gate of vitality) point, holds a large part of the body's energy.

For these two points to be activated, the hips must be relaxed. The legs should be light but allow for constant movement.

The posture should be controlled and can begin with some simple preparatory movements that are executed before every practice for fifteen to thirty minutes. Most professionals advise students to begin with the upper-body exercises and then move down to the feet.

The Head

Extend the head up, like a turtle leaving its shell. Then lock the neck between the shoulders and stretch it until it feels like the top of the head is suspended from the sky. Repeat three sets of this exercise nine times.

Turn the head to the right and left, keeping alignment with the whole spine. Move the body like a crane, with the feet stable and the arms, torso, and head together.

The Eyes

Concentrate on a point close by and then slowly focus on farther points, working to shift your attention. At first, perform the exercise twenty times per minute, and eventually forty times per minute when you're better trained.

To concentrate the attention inward, squint your eyes as if you're angry and slowly focus your gaze as if you suspected someone of something. Repeat the exercise three times. While performing tai chi, always look just a meter in front of you.

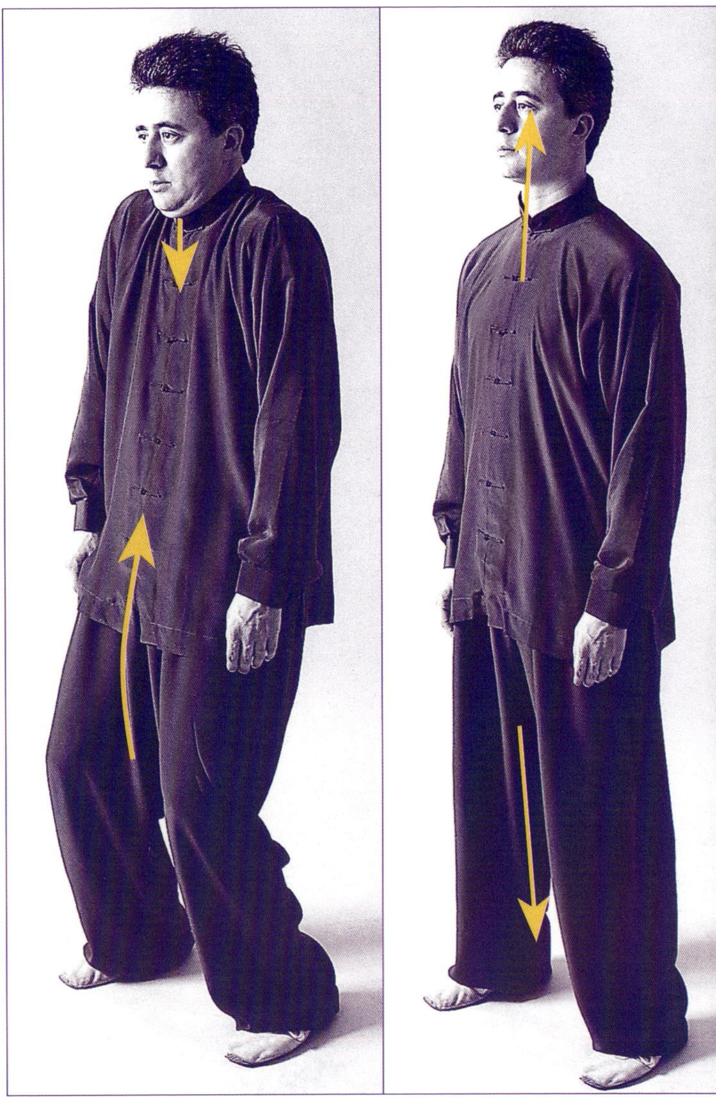

Don't focus on close objects, like the hands, or far objects, like the horizon.

The Shoulders

To start, move the shoulders forward and backward with small rotations, as if trying to draw circles. Perform this rotation nine times with each shoulder. Place a hand over the shoulder during the exercise to feel your shoulder move, not your back.

The Abdominal Region

Make circles with your hips in all directions, as if you were using a hula hoop. Repeat the exercise, trying to make circles deeper, without moving the hips. First practice the motions on a horizontal plane and afterward vertically, ten minutes each time.

The Spinal Column

Vertically align all of the vertebrae. Make vertical circles forward and backward, as if the body were a windblown reed, soft and secure. Close the hips, bringing them in toward the sacrum, reducing the tension on the back.

The Chest and the Back

Open and close the hands on either side of your body,

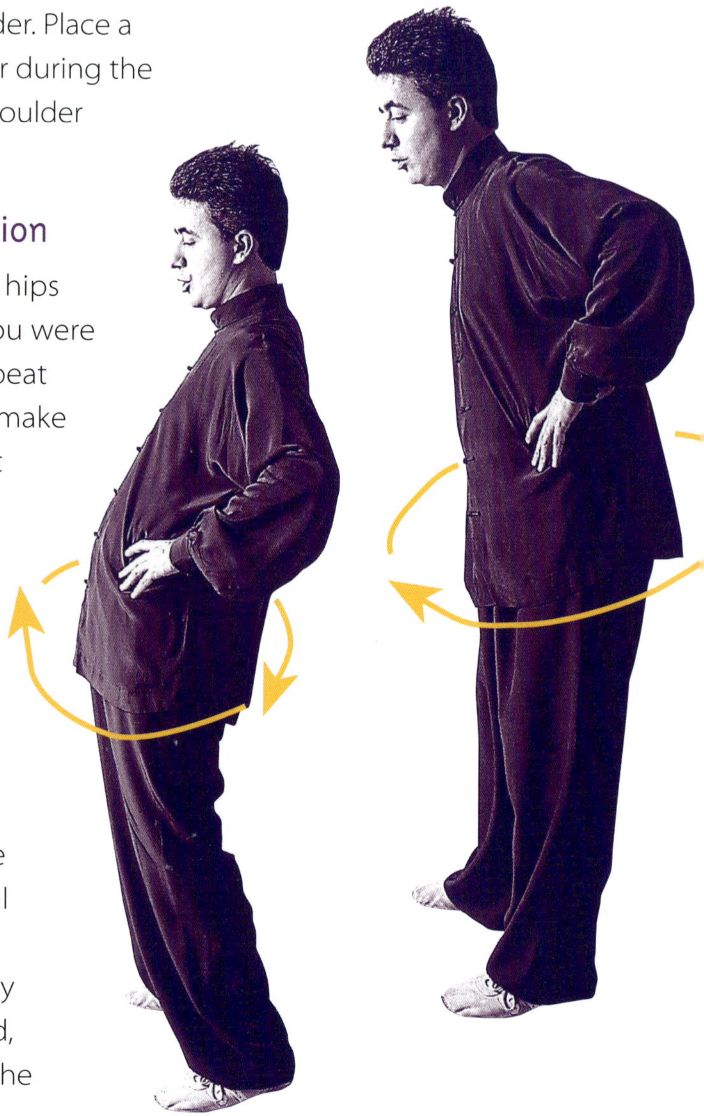

bringing the backs of the palms backward and opening the chest wide. Now bend forward, moving your chest inward. The first few times you practice this, press the breastbone with the palm of the hand to help the curvature of the chest.

The Hips

Place your hands one on top of the other, move them to the top of your head, and turn your hips left and right.

The Legs and Feet

Alternate lifting your knees, as if a cushion was blown up underneath your feet. Imagine that you step on the cushion while you lift the other leg, which will increase stability and eliminate fatigue.

The Fundamental Postures

Now that we have discussed the warm-up exercises, it's time to consider the fundamental postures of immobile feet. After this, we'll move on to the forms of walking without using the arms, and finish with the complete movements that make up the diverse sequences of tai chi. Here, only the form of Twenty-Four Movements is analyzed, illustrated in the chapter "The Twenty-Four Tai Chi Movements" (page 52). The order in which the postures are explained reproduces the normal sequence of training.

Static Postures

CHI LI (The Upright Posture)

This is the initial posture for all tai chi forms: the open feet should be shoulder-width distance apart, with the weight evenly distributed and the heels squarely on the floor. Many people stand in an improper upright position by centering the weight to the front or side of the foot. Balance a book on your head in front of a mirror to see if your weight is centered.

To know if some point of the foot is receiving more pressure than the other points, take a look at one of your old shoes and note the areas of wear on the sole. If it's evenly worn out, your general posture is balanced. If it's not, the part of the shoe that is most worn out is where you place most of your weight.

TING BU (The T-Posture)

Beginning with the previous posture, switch the weight from one foot to the other. This changes the situation from balancing on two feet to moving all the pressure to one foot and freeing the other. Practice the two parts, bringing the weight first to the left and then to the right, keeping the head held by the top to the sky and controlling your center of gravity (tan tien). Always keep your back straight. This position is called the T-Position because the foot with the "full" weight is stopped, while the other "empty" foot supports the point on the ground, the heel turned inward to form a T with the other foot. This makes a transitional posture used in the yin phase.

GONG BU (The Bow)

This is one of the fundamental postures of tai chi. To perform it, start in the initial position with the legs open and take a step forward so that the back leg is extended with the point of the foot turning 45° to the outside, while the front leg is bent. During the motion, always shift the weight from the forward-moving foot to support the heel first and then the sole. Press forcefully on the floor with both feet in this position and move forward with the trunk.

At the end of the exercise, the weight is distributed 60 percent on the bent leg and 40 percent on the distended leg. Perform the displacement in front of both legs and, when they are secure, repeat the exercise to the left and right, consecutively connecting the indications of the starting position of *chi li* and of the transitional position of *ting bu.*

XU BU (The Empty Posture)

This posture is called "empty," or "false," because the front foot does not support the weight. Starting at the left *gong bu* position, move the back foot forward and reduce the distance halfway to the front. First support the point of the foot, then the sole, and lift the leg forward. The result is a high position in which the foot behind the front foot has the point turned 45° out, while the front foot is lifted, with the point or heel supported on the floor; the two heels are aligned.

ZUO BU (Sitting Backward)

From the previous posture, bring the "empty" foot back, as if you were walking on a railing, first supporting the point of the foot and then the entire sole, which should be turned out 45°. In the final position, the weight is distributed 60 percent on the back foot and 40 percent on the front foot. The feeling is like sitting backward, keeping the body's center of gravity above the feet. The head or the buttocks are often too far backward, which causes a loss of stability.

MA BU (The Horse)

This posture is used to walk to the side. From the exit posture of chi li, move one foot to the side until both are separated at double the width of the shoulders. Move the knees forward—thus lowering the bust—to position yourself as if riding a horse. The feet are parallel, and the weight is distributed equally above them; the torso is centered. For the movements from the center to the side and vice versa, always perform the process of emptying and filling. In this position, it is best not to lower down too far at first, because it's easy to bring the weight to the knees rather than the heels, placing pressure on the joints. The knee should not go past the foot or converge inward.

DU LI BU (Above a Foot)

This posture is also called the rooster, referring to the way a rooster stands. From this initial posture, alternate lifting each knee and stay balanced on one foot, with the toes of the other foot pointing down. Normally, this is used as a step into the next posture.

PU BU (Low Posture)

From the initial posture, lift the left knee, staying balanced on the right foot. Move the right knee forward, bending it down and lowering the body with the left leg extended to the left. Repeat this exercise in both directions, trying to keep the body erect and lowering until the buttocks almost touch the ground.

Moving or Walking Postures

"WALKING TAI CHI," MOVEMENT FORWARD

This movement is performed from the Bow position on the left, *zuo gong bu*, to arrive at the posture to the right, *you gong bu*.

From zuo gong bu, move your weight backward onto the right leg, raising the point of the left foot and turning it 45° to the left.

Now, supporting the entire sole of the left foot, move forward with the right foot, keeping the point close to the inner part of the other foot. In this position, move a step forward with the right foot, first supporting the heel and then the entire sole. At this point you have reached you gong bu. Walk backward while following these instructions in the opposite direction; be sure to move slowly, always keeping your head at the same height and your body shifted to the right.

"REPULSE MONKEY," MOVEMENT BACKWARD

The feet stay parallel as if moving on rails. Perform the step of the left posture zuo bu (see page 32) with the left foot back. First moving the point, and then the heel of the foot, move the right leg, taking a few steps back.

"WALK BETWEEN CLOUDS," LATERAL MOVEMENT

Begin from the Horse position (see page 33) and move the right foot to the left, situating it more or less two feet to the left. To perform the movement, pay attention to the emptying and filling of the foot and support the point of the foot first and the sole after. After moving the right foot, move the left foot to the left, returning to the Horse position in this manner. Repeat this walk to the right and left; for the form of Twenty-Four Movements, the walk should always go to the left.

The Three Coordinations

Once students have mastered the fundamental postures and walks of tai chi, they must train what are called the three coordinations. To perform this training, one starts from the principle that the different parts of the body should move according to precise rules. One of these rules is to understand how to coordinate the top and bottom parts of the body at every moment. Other rules include:

- How the hand corresponds with the foot
- How the elbow corresponds with the knee
- How the shoulders correspond with the hips

In every position, the movements generated by the torso, tan tien, are transferred to the legs and arms, arriving at the feet and hands at the same time.

One must be sure to always maintain the three coordinations by looking in a mirror and comparing one's positioning with the examples in this book. Often, after having

performed a posture, the hand is not positioned in line with the foot, but rather more forward or behind. This sometimes happens with the elbows as well—when they are positioned too close or too far away from the body. The body should experience a feeling of fullness and continuity of movement, which will be lost if any interruption or imbalance occurs. If you feel unbalanced or falter during the execution, it is better to stop and repeat the exercise from the beginning to improve the unity of the motion.

The harmony is transmitted to every muscle, ligament, and bone of the body. Sometimes the hands can shrink back too fast, before the movement reaches the shoulders, or the ligaments of the hands become tense.

It's necessary to train the exercises of the tai chi motions, combining them with typical hand motions of this form: this confers more harmony between the different parts of the body and increases the knowledge of one's own energy.

Breathing, Relaxation, and Circulation of Chi

This chapter shows how to breathe correctly and in a controlled manner, a practice called *tiao chi*, which can improve the practice of tai chi. You'll also find illustrations of the most appropriate exercises to help develop the consciousness of the circulation of chi, called *chi kung* (chi work). These are exercises frequently used by masters to help move the energy of the body before performing the tai chi movements.

Breathing

At first you don't have to worry about how to breathe, but more about improving the quality of the movements and exercising the postures of the three coordinations. While practicing tai chi, breathing has to be natural. Natural means not forcing anything, neither breaths too large nor breaths too short. It's necessary that we concentrate on the breath to make it regular and constant. One must always remember that.

It also happens that at a certain age, breaths become shorter as the intercostal muscles and diaphragm lose efficiency. According to Chinese culture, the body does not only receive nutrition from food, but also from energy,

I y Chi, "the intention recharges our chi."

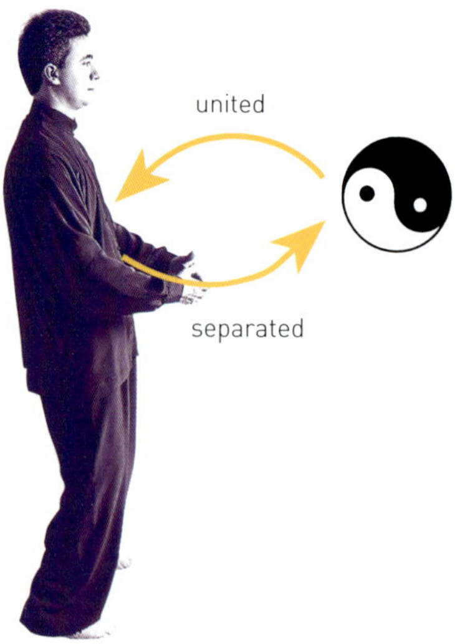

During inhalation, the air that enters the lungs unites with the air that leaves the tan tien. Once the positive energy is absorbed, the negative energy leaves the body through dilation of the abdomen.

yang, which it takes from the universe through breathing. When the body receives energy, it also eliminates negative energy, yin, with every exhalation.

Normally, only 10 percent of the air in the lungs is exchanged during a breathing cycle, and this percentage only decreases as we age.

To increase this percentage, abdominal, or inverse, breathing must be practiced. This breathing is also called fetal breathing because it is the way that a fetus gets air from the mother, or Taoist breathing due to the monks' use of it during training techniques for longevity. This type of breathing soothes the entire organism and transmits a greater inner calm, which is an indispensible asset for all tai chi students. To exercise this type of breathing, you can perform the exercise called *ti bao shi* (sustaining the ball) in the abdomen.

Stand comfortably upright and imagine you are holding a large ball in front of the abdomen. As you inhale, imagine absorbing the ball through the belly button and picture it inflating while you expand the abdomen.

Another exercise that is very useful consists of imagining that you are pushing a car or lifting a great weight. The abdomen expands due to the force, utilizing the type of breathing we want to practice.

A particularly useful breath for older masters is the turtle breath, which gets its name from an animal characterized by its longevity.

This breathing consists of reducing the rhythm of inhalation and exhalation as much as possible, going from fourteen or fifteen breaths per minute to about three, and thus practicing inverse breathing.

To do this, you need to practice every tai chi movement as slowly as possible, without interrupting the breathing.

In this way, we can achieve a better general state of health and reinforce our immune system.

Root Exercises

In order for the practice of the tai chi exercises not to result in a purely empty sequence, you also have to think about energy in order to enjoy the tangible benefits of the improvement of your skill and general heath.

It's easy to understand how the universe around us influences our own being when you think about how a sunny day fills us with lively happiness while an overcast or rainy day makes us sad.

According to Chinese culture, all phenomena are explained by the fact that each human being, as we have already noted, is part of an integrated universe, according to the principles of yin and yang.

Whe practicing tai chi, it is of utmost importance to harmonize these energies. The first energy is the ability to feel the earth: the classic texts affirm that the energy accumulated in the tan tien is a combination of energy taken from the earth and energy taken from the sky.

This can be understood considering that, even standing on our feet, we do not come into full contact with the ground because our attention is not directed downward.

In effect, if one concentrates too much on coordinating the movements of the arms, one forgets about the roots. Because of this, the body should act from within itself to maintain balance. There are exercises called "from the root," because they improve stability and help one perceive the energy of the earth.

After placing yourself in the first position, chi li (see page 30), concentrate on the feet (which are like the roots of a tree) and press the heels into the ground, helping yourself with arm rotations from the top downward. After repeating these presses twenty times, relax and lift the legs as if to walk. Anyone who has leg problems, like swelling or varicose veins, should perform these exercises even more slowly.

Body Relaxation

Before beginning the tai chi movements, we should have the body and mind ready and, above all, relaxed. When that is achieved, we can start with some exercises called *chan su chin* (from the silk cocoon). First we relax every muscle, slowly concentrating on the different parts of the body, beginning with the head until we arrive at the toes. Then we can begin the chi regulation exercises.

Bring the hands up and then forward and down, very slowly with the palms facing down. Repeat this nine times. Later, move on to perform rotations of all the joints of the body, beginning with the wrists, elbows,

and shoulders, and then lowering down to the buttocks and legs. You can perform horizontal rotations of the buttocks, head, knees, and spine, first clockwise and then counterclockwise. Later, follow the symbol of the yin and yang with vertical rotations and in a figure eight, using every part of the body, including the internal organs.

Another useful body-relaxing exercise consists of imitating the movements of animals when they dry their wet fur: without contracting any muscles, shake yourself in every direction.

After practicing these exercises for a few minutes, it's useful to concentrate on the tan tien to tighten the different parts that have been relaxed.

The Development of Chi

Through constant practice of tai chi, we begin to feel the increase and decrease of the chi in the body. This is a difficult aspect to train and especially difficult to understand in the West. However, students with advanced skill training will be able to hone these skills.

The first exercise consists of teaching the mind to feel the chi and the direction it flows during the exercises. The main goal is to take and free this energy. There are key points in the body to be considered:

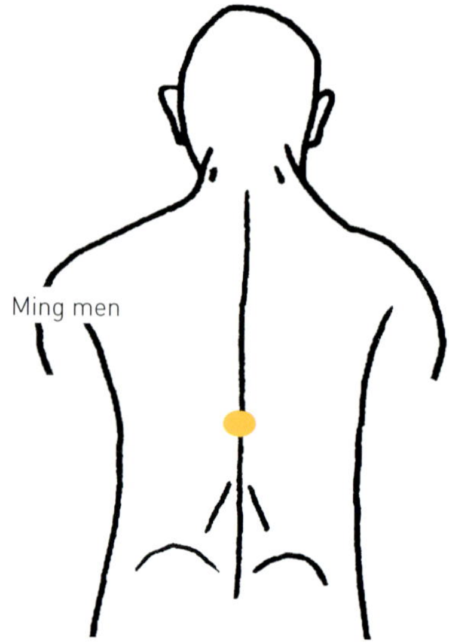

- The lower tan tien (*qihai*), four fingers below the belly button

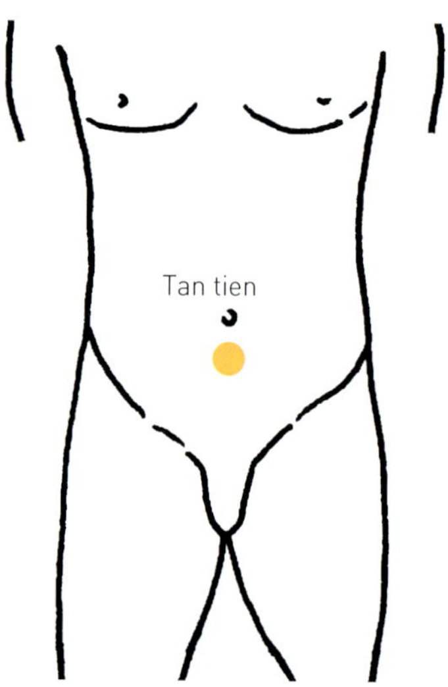

- The *baihui*, the center of the head, at the junction of all cranial bones
- The *gao wang* for men and *huiyin* for women, located in the genital regions
- The *laogong* and the *yongquan*, which are situated in the center of the hand and foot, respectively

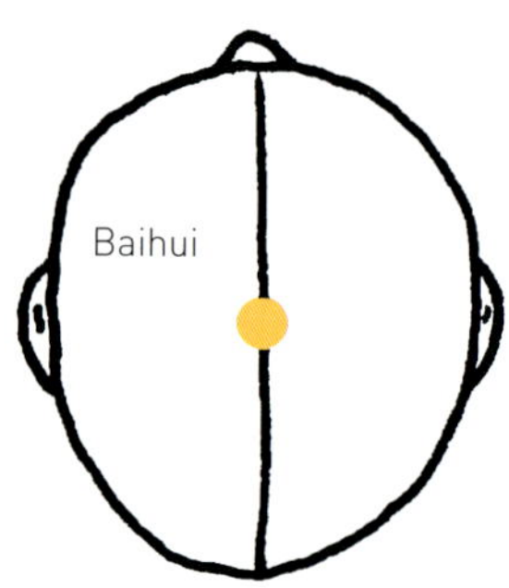

- The *ming men* (gate of vitality), situated on the back, close to the fourteenth vertebra
- The *yuzhen*, the point between the first vertebra and the cranium.

Learning about these key points helps students locate them and visualize how the chi should flow through the body. The most popular visualization exercise is called the small circulation. It serves to maintain the mind in a calm, stable state. One must concentrate on uniting first the baihui point with the lower tan tien (qihai), passing down the *yintang* and *shan zhong* points, then the qihai with the gao wang and the gao wang with the ming men points. Finally, the student mentally passes through the *lingtai* and yuzhen points to reach the baihui point again, thus completing the circulation. It is fundamental to follow this sequence to achieve good results.

In tai chi, this circuit of energy should be united with the physical movements only after you can perform this technique perfectly.

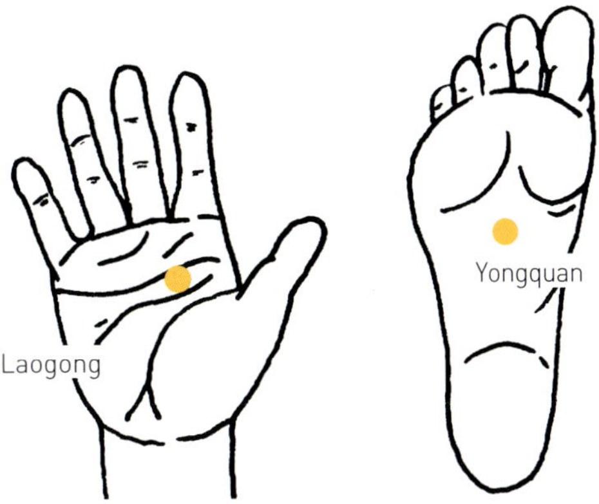

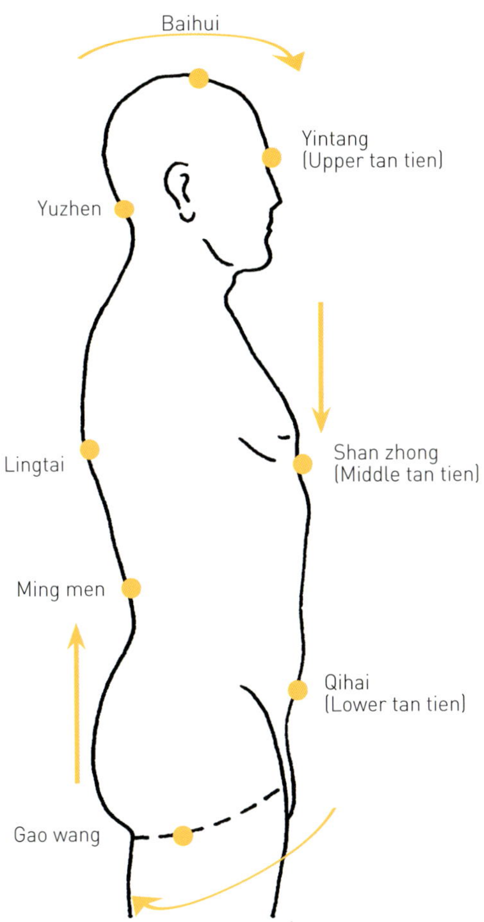

This is a model of the xiao zhou tian or "small circulation," including the tan tien and the most important areas of the body with respect to the chi. The arrows indicate the direction of the circulation of the chi.

The Master Responds

This chapter addresses questions that students and interested people have formulated and presented to the author during his twenty years of experience teaching tai chi.

Why is tai chi written in so many different ways?

Taiji quan is the proper spelling used throughout China, after the government's introduction of the Pinyin alphabet (the official Chinese transliteration system).

Before that, the term "tai chi chuan" was used, which was also written in various ways and is still widely used in Taiwan and the United States.

Throughout the East, the term "taiji quan" has experienced variations depending on the country.

Tan tien jing, "the essence is in the tai chi."

The Different Forms of the Name "Tai Chi"

The term "tai chi" varies throughout the world. The current form is "taiji quan," but "tai chi chuan" is often used.

The following are other known variations:

- T'ai chi ch'üan
- T'ai ki k'iuan
- Tai ji meng
- Tai ki
- Tai ki kiuan
- Tai ki tchuan
- Tai ki tsiuan
- Tai kic kuen
- Tai kik
- Tai kik kuen
- Tai kik pai
- Tai kit kuen

What are the differences between modern and traditional tai chi?

Tai chi is an age-old art, spread from ancient eras, and because of that, it has experienced a constant evolution. The most important change was, without a doubt, produced after the Cultural Revolution. During this period, more conservative expressions of Chinese culture were eliminated, like religion, some cultural traditions, and martial arts.

However, today in China, modern tai chi is studied in gyms, and it's different from the traditional or orthodox forms because of its emphasis on the more graceful and smoother movements of the discipline. Modern tai chi does not focus on the effective application of the techniques in combat, which is actually the most significant part of traditional tai chi.

What are the differences between tai chi and chi kung?

In tai chi the consciousness exercises lead to the expression of the technique as self-defense. Chi kung consists of a series of techniques with the sole objective of improving health by combining circular movements with inner breathing. It is undeniable that in tai chi all of the fundamental techniques should contain specific chi kung techniques to optimize the accumulation of energy and emission of force.

At what age should people start practicing tai chi?

No age has been determined to be the best to start practicing tai chi. Many of my students have started after their fifties and, in spite of this, have achieved incredible fluency. Some students have even started practicing at the age of seventy. If you wish to gain combat fluency, however, it is better to begin when you are between twenty and thirty years old.

What practical benefits can be seen after a year of tai chi practice?

Practicioners will immediately pay closer attention to their own movements, like how they walk and breathe. They will improve their fluidity and body relaxation.

This is enough to alleviate joint pain in the body, caused by a lack of specific movement, and eliminate stress and internal tension. From the practice of tai chi, one can obtain a normalization of health and at least help prevent the onset of some psychosomatic diseases.

Is it obligatory to learn the martial part?

To be able to practice tai chi, it's not always necessary to learn to defend yourself. What counts the most is moving your own chi properly.

Whoever wants to have a more complete perception and visualization of their own results has to learn the techniques and corresponding applications. Students can train in pairs in order to learn about the more diverse forces and aspects that make up tai chi.

What is chi, and how is it possible to feel it?

Chi is in all living beings. It is what makes them live. There are three types of chi: the natural chi (also called the celestial chi), the terrestrial chi (derived from food), and the light chi (also called the chi of the five organs). This last chi (light chi) is found in the body and often called *zhen chi* as well.

Tai chi tries to maintain and develop this latter chi. By trying to walk, breathe, and move appropriately and following the rules regulating the yin and yang, this stimulates the maintenance of energy in the body, along with the benefits of the chi.

After practicing tai chi exercises, many people have a sensation of a hot liquid moving through their bodies; others feel a current provoking light shivering in its wake.

When and where should tai chi be practiced?

Normally, the best moment to practice is at sunrise, when there's more chi growth from nature (*da zi ran ji chi*).

While it's also possible to practice at any other part of the day, it's best to avoid windy or cloudy days.

The best places to practice are where you feel rejuvenated, like in parks and gardens, and especially close to large trees. But in general, any quiet place where you will not be bothered and you can focus your mind is good.

Why is tai chi considered an internal style?

Tai chi is not just made of slow muscle movements. It also uses other structures, like bones and ligaments, which contribute to the growth of movement and, combined with the will, to the movement of chi through the body.

What does 'i' mean?

I, "will," is the primary and essential spring of power that moves one's intention. Without it, one can have the desire to perform a particular action but not be able to put it into practice. For example, if we have a pot full of water on the stove, we can turn on the gas (chi), but without the will to light a match (i), the water will never boil. This means that practicing tai chi is not enough. We also have to keep intention in our mind and constantly maintain all the techniques.

How is it possible to train without a teacher?

If someone has the intention to learn, it is not necessary to follow a teacher. Practicing with a good manual is a great way to learn the basics. For starters, one can follow these key rules: warm up with preparatory movements to free the channels; exercise the basic walks and movements to help the fluidity of the techniques; make just one movement and repeat it to learn the sequence; move to the next movement only after mastering the previous one; always repeat movements from the beginning without interruptions; concentrate and avoid other thoughts; and disconnect electrical appliances (radio, television, cell phones, etc.) that can distract you from your training. To be able to progress and understand if the actions are done correctly, it's sometimes necessary to be advised by a more experienced person. This does not, however, invalidate daily personal training.

Which is the best among all the tai chi styles?

Nobody can say one style is better than the others, nor should anyone believe that his or her preferred style is better. In fact, differences among styles only exist in the expression of the energy. When practiced well, all of the different types of tai chi create a unique jewel. It's possible to practice many different styles but to execute them superficially and without merit. We should not search for the best style, but rather our own. This way, we do not close ourselves off to external experiences and always remain open to exchanges. A certain teacher or style should never be rejected. It's better to try to understand why the differences exist so that, if we find some aspects of a variant style useful, we can enrich our overall experience of tai chi.

What distinguishes the substantial from the nonsubstantial?

During tai chi practice, the entire body moves as if submerged in a thick liquid. The student should feel the change in the weight of one foot or the other, distinguishing between the "full/empty" alternations. In effect, full (*shi*) and empty (*xu*) are two concepts that must be trained.

A rigid body is shi, and its movements are difficult, discontinuous, and tense, aware of the possibility of losing balance. At the same time, a body that is too xu does not have vitality and loses the ability to maintain a good flow of chi. Normally, somebody who is too xu has a rigid chest and high shoulders, while someone who is too shi has a lowered head and inconsistent movements.

Why do some students wear a white uniform and others a black or blue one?

Unlike in Japan and other countries, there is less of an emphasis on the standardization of uniforms in China. They serve to distinguish one school from another, and their design depends a lot on the personal aesthetic of the founder, who decides to choose one color over another. This being said, there are three types of uniforms that have found widespread popularity: the white one, used by participants in modern tai chi competitions; the black one, used by traditionalists; and the blue uniform, the Taoist color employed in the schools that study the internal styles and focus on building a path to the *tao*. Normally, the classic uniform includes Chinese buttons and is open in the front, but these days, during practical training, sports outfits and cotton jackets are used. What's important is that the uniforms are comfortable and allow for free-flowing movements.

Many people practice tai chi for their health, and others for competition. Which is better?

I believe that any reason that encourages the practice of tai chi is valid; there is no one reason that has priority over the others or makes them less valuable. Students will greatly benefit from opening themselves up to the different experiences tai chi can provide, rather than becoming fixated on a singular objective.

Many tai chi students do not find competition or combat a necessary experience; naturally, there is actually no obligation to pursue either, but one should be aware of all the possibilities tai chi offers without rejection or prejudice.

For example, one can practice in parks without being worried about what other people will think, or participate in a competition without their objective being to win. With this disposition, students can improve their tai chi practice greatly.

The Twenty-Four Tai Chi Movements

The Simplified Taiji Quan, also called Tai Chi of Twenty-Four Movements, has been devised by the Chinese commission with the goal of codifying it and spreading it throughout the world. This form of tai chi consists of twenty different movements extracted from the larger sequence of the Yang style. Three of these are performed to the right and left, and one is repeated twice. Therefore, there are twenty-four movements in total. To practice this form, it is best to face the south, following the diagram on page 54.

The diagram is a conventional representation of the succession of the movements; it is a map of evolutions. The movements are performed along the same line and displaced laterally. It's important to note the point where the first movements are performed, because it will also be the place to perform the last movements. One should begin and end with the opening and

Tai chi, "supreme movement."

closing movements, concentrating on the tan tien. Following these instructions, the student must concentrate on every motion. Every move should be repeated at least thirty-six times. When the student has repeated all of the movements of a section, these movements should be done once again all together. Afterward, all sections should be repeated together until the student reaches the eighth section, thus performing all twenty-four movements.

The sequence of the movements should not be interrupted. If, during the execution of the forms, there are pauses, start again from the beginning. The breathing should be natural and relaxed.

Once a series is learned, breathe with the abdomen, keeping the chest and lungs relaxed. When the necessary practice has been achieved, the complete series can be performed in about five minutes.

Instructions for Following the Explanations and Reading the Diagram

In the explanations of the images, the movements are analyzed according to the sequence of gestures. Because of this, it is important that these are executed well and without modifications. The explanation begins with the position of the feet, followed by the movements of the rest of the body, and ends with the hands.

The series is described in the space, taking the four cardinal points as a reference. Begin facing south, since every subsequent direction refers to this initial one.

In the images, the continuous line indicates the trajectory of the right foot or hand, while the dotted line refers to the left foot or hand. The arrows indicate the placement of the hands and feet for the following figure.

Keep in mind that the arrows and lines, while rather accurate, only indicate the approximate trajectory of the movement.

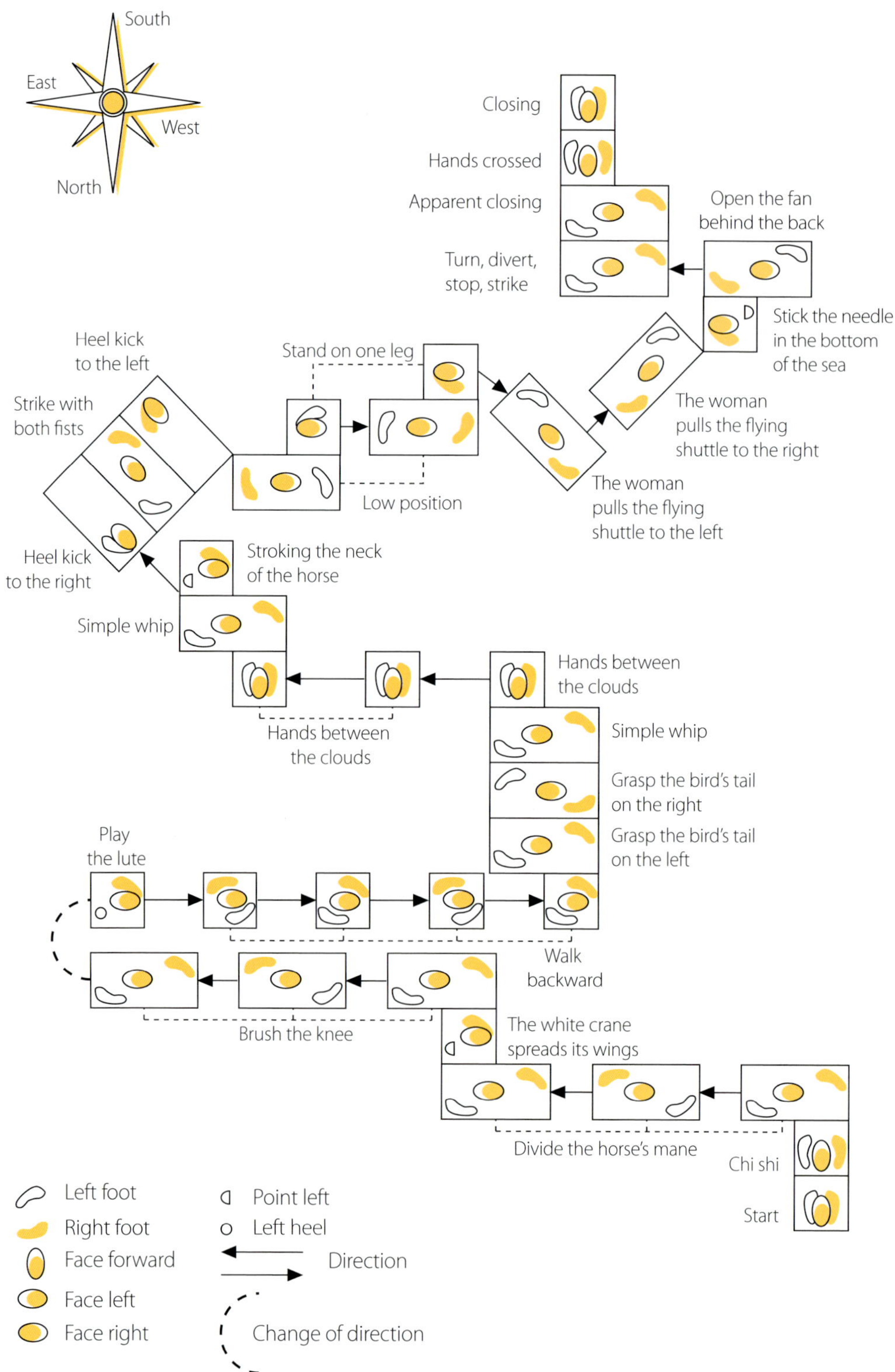
South
East
West
North
Closing
Hands crossed
Apparent closing
Open the fan
behind the back
Turn, divert,
stop, strike
Stick the needle
in the bottom
of the sea
Heel kick
to the left
Stand on one leg
Strike with
both fists
The woman
pulls the flying
shuttle to the right
Low position
The woman
pulls the flying
shuttle to the left
Heel kick
to the right
Stroking the neck
of the horse
Simple whip
Hands between
the clouds
Hands between
the clouds
Simple whip
Grasp the bird's tail
on the right
Play
the lute
Grasp the bird's tail
on the left
Walk
backward
Brush the knee
The white crane
spreads its wings
Divide the horse's mane
Chi shi
Start
Left foot
Right foot
Face forward
Face left
Face right
Point left
Left heel
Direction
Change of direction

The Execution of the Movements

Chinese name: *Yu bei* (Preparation).

Preparation: Face south with your feet together, your body erect with arms by your sides, legs slightly bent, looking forward, tongue touching your palate, and making sure to breathe freely and naturally.

Taoist references:
Concentrate on the tan tien in the *wu chi* position.

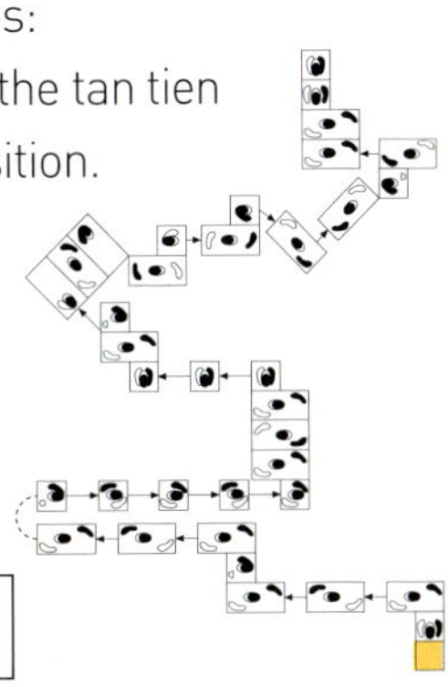

First Section

MOVEMENT 1

Chinese name: *Chi shi* (Starting Movement), postures 1 to 4.

Posture 1: Separate the feet (chi li). Bring the majority of the body weight to the right foot. Move your weight from the left to the right, supporting the point of the foot on the ground and then the sole. Your arms should be by your sides.

Breathing: Inhale as you lift the left foot and exhale as you support it on the floor.

Taoist references: Passing from the wu chi state to tai chi.

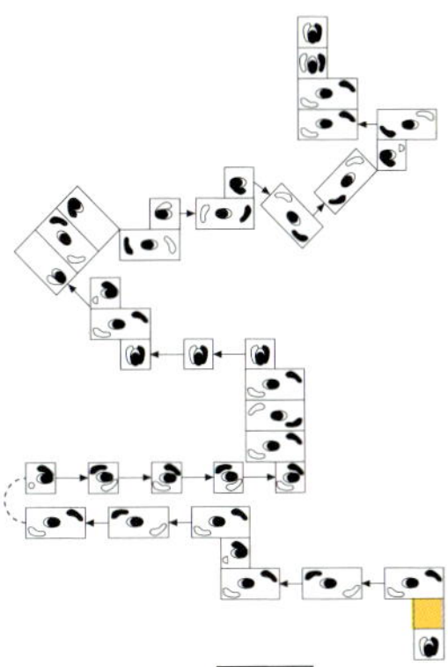

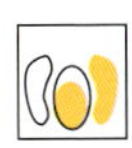

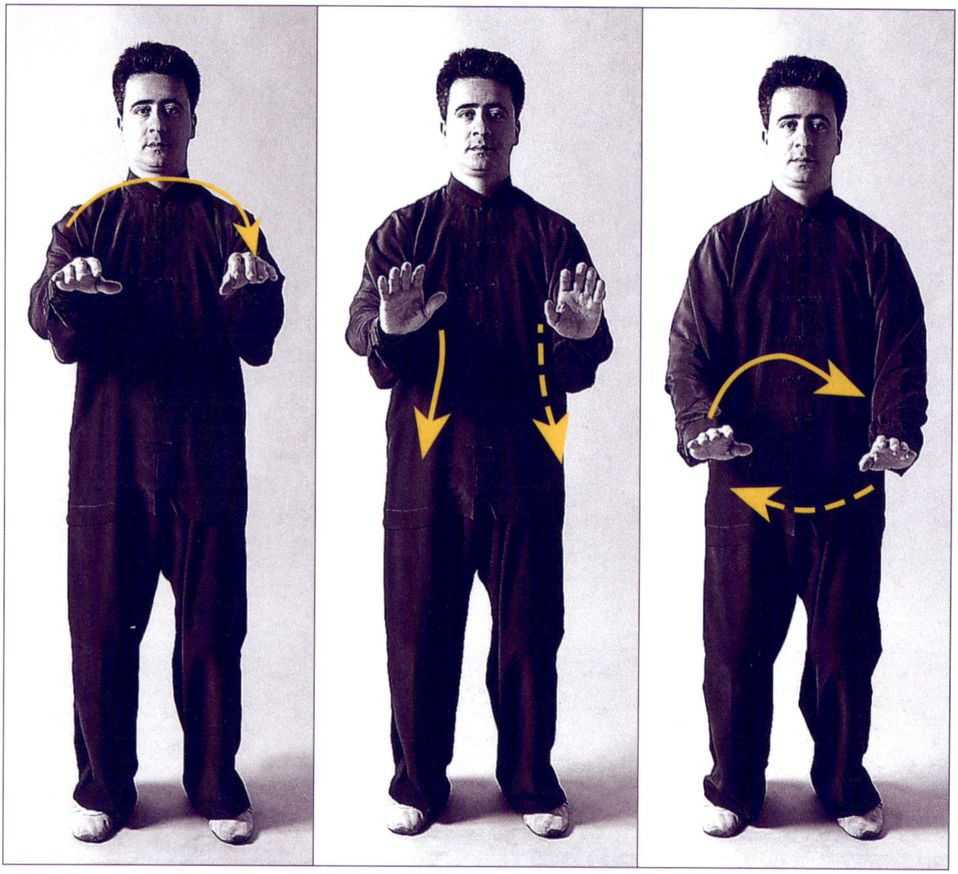

Posture 2: Lift the arms slowly to the level of your shoulders, being careful not to raise them further. Your elbows, palms, and fingers face down.

Posture 3: Lift your fingertips with the palms facing forward.

Breathing: Exhaling.

Essence of the technique: Use the jijing force (see page 22), passing the strength to your fingertips.

Posture 4: Lower your hands down to the belly button while you move the knees forward.

Breathing: Exhaling.

Essence of the technique: Lowering, first using the lujing force (see page 21), to concentrate on the tan tien point, and then pressing with the jijing force in the laogong and yongquan points.

MOVEMENT 2

Chinese name: *Zuo you ye ma fen zong* (Parting the Wild Horse's Mane), postures 5 to 19.

Posture 5 (left part):
Turn your head right (southeast), bringing the left hand down to the right, as if holding a ball between your hands close to the right side while simultaneously moving your weight to the right foot.

Breathing: Inhaling.

Posture 6 (left part):
At the same time as the hands, move the left foot to the right (west), focusing your center of gravity to the point on the ground. Don't move your hips and keep the head and body straight.

Breathing: Finish the breathing.

Posture 7 (left part):
Move the left foot to the east with the point lifted and bring the right hand down and the left up.

Breathing: Exhaling.

Posture 8 (left part):
First, support your heel and then slowly support your whole left foot. At the same time move the hands, as if caressing and dividing a horse's mane; the right hand goes down while the left hand goes up. Perform the movements at the same time; the hands and legs should stop at the same time as well.

Breathing:
Continue exhaling.

Posture 9 (left part):
Bring the weight of the body forward, performing gong bu (see page 31).
In the final position, the left arm is in front of the body, the left elbow is perpendicular to the knee, and the left hand is placed slightly to the right but not in front of the face. The right hand is separated about six inches (about fifteen centimeters) from the thigh.

Breathing:
Finish exhaling.

Posture 10 (right part):
Bring your weight to the right foot while you lift the left, beginning a rotation with the body to the northeast.

Breathing: Inhaling.
Essence of the technique:
Use the liejing force (see page 23), acting as if you are dividing something.

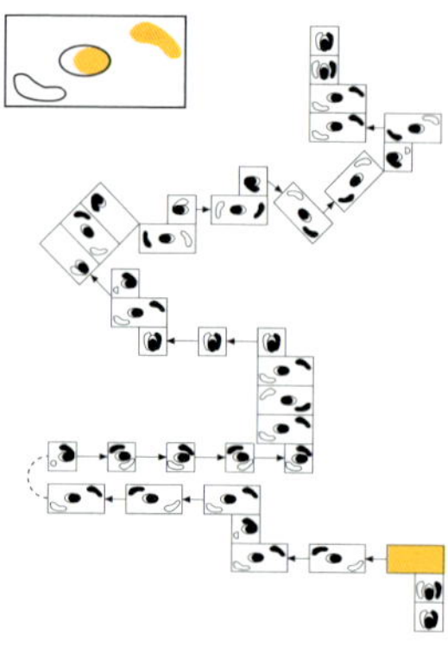

Posture 11 (right part):
Continue turning the body to the northeast, bringing the right hand down to the left and, at the same time, bringing the weight to the left foot.

Breathing: Continue inhaling.

Posture 12 (right part): First move the right foot forward, supporting it in the ting bu position (see page 31). Continue the movement with the right hand below the left, as if holding a ball.

Breathing: Finish inhaling.

Posture 13 (right part): Move the right foot to the east, support the heel, and begin to move the left hand down and the right one up.

Breathing: Exhaling.

Posture 14 (right part): First support the heel and then slowly support the whole foot. Bring the whole body weight over it, in the gong bu position. Simultaneously, think about caressing and dividing a horse's mane, lowering with the left hand and raising with the right one. In the final position, the right hand is in front and the left on the left thigh.

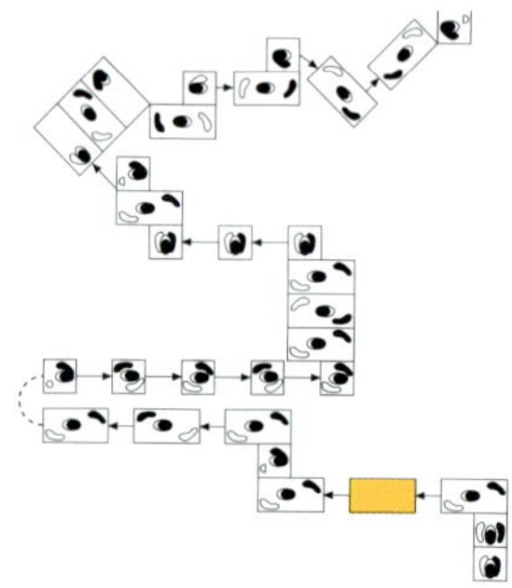

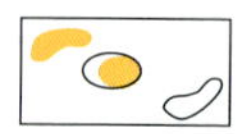

Breathing: Continue exhaling.

Essence of the technique: Use the liejing force as if you were going to divide something.

Posture 15 (left part): Bring your weight onto the left foot and lift the right foot, beginning a rotational movement southeast.

Breathing: Inhaling.

Posture 16 (left part): Turn to the southeast, bringing the left hand down below the right as if moving a ball. At the same time, move the weight onto the right foot.

Breathing: Continue inhaling.

Posture 17 (left part):
Bring the left foot to the front, supporting it on the point in the ting bu position. Continue the movement with the left hand below the right, as if holding a ball.

Breathing:
Finish inhaling.

Posture 18 (left part):
Perform the eighth posture, including the breathing.

Posture 19 (left part):
Perform the ninth posture, including the breathing.

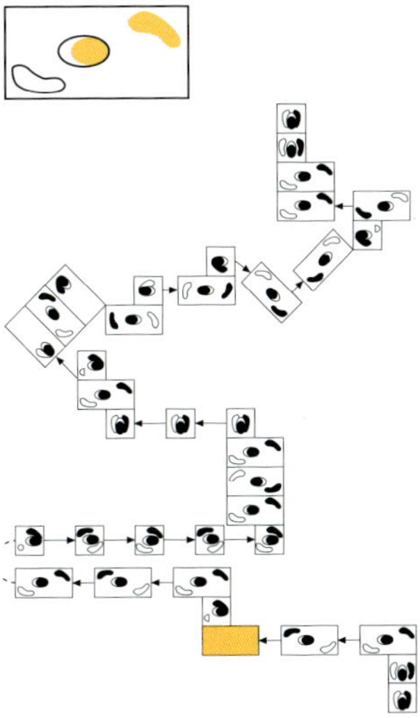

MOVEMENT 3

Chinese name: *Bai he liang chi* (White Crane Spreads Its Wings), postures 20 to 22. This movement is the shortest in the first section.

Posture 20: With the weight on the left foot, perform an empty step with the right, *xu bu* (see page 32), bringing it half a step forward and supporting the point of the foot on the floor. At the same time, bring the right hand below the left, as if holding a ball.

Breathing: Inhaling.

Posture 21: Support the heel of the right foot and take a step back, keeping the body straight and beginning to open the hands. The left hand goes down (north) and the right goes up (south).

Breathing: Exhaling.

Posture 22: With the weight on the right foot, open the arms, as if they were the wings of a crane. The left hand is in front of the body, palm facing down and about eight inches to the side, while the right hand is at eye level, with the palm facing inward.

Breathing: Finish inhaling.
Essence of the technique: Use the pengjing force (see page 21) to expand, as if growing.

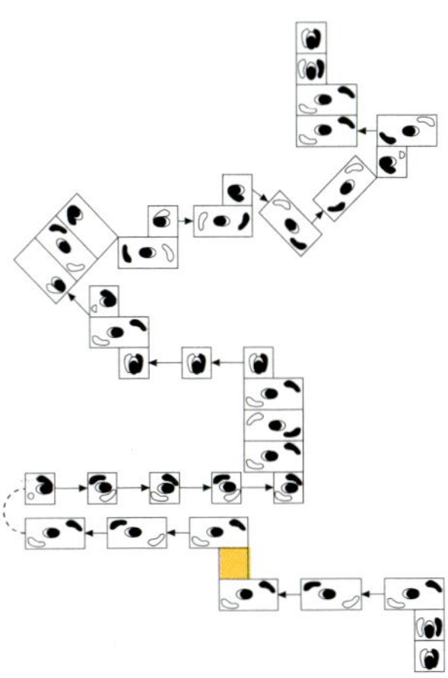

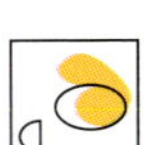

Second Section

MOVEMENT 4

Chinese name: *Zou you lou xi ao bu* (Brush Knee Right and Twist Step), postures 23 to 37.

Posture 23: Turning the hips northeast, move the right hand and perform a stop, passing it in front of the face and, while continuing the movement northeast, draw a semicircle downward.

Breathing: Inhaling.

Posture 24: Turn the hips southeast and move the left hand to perform a stop, passing it in front of the face. Draw a semicircle downward while continuing the movement to the southeast.

Breathing: Inhaling.

Posture 25: Look toward the southeast, lifting the right hand up to eye level. Meanwhile, the left hand passes in front of the abdomen, parallel to the floor.

Breathing: Finish inhaling.

Posture 26 (left part): Move the left foot to the east, moving the point forward and supporting the heel after. Move your right hand close to the face, pushing out and to the front.

Breathing: Exhaling.

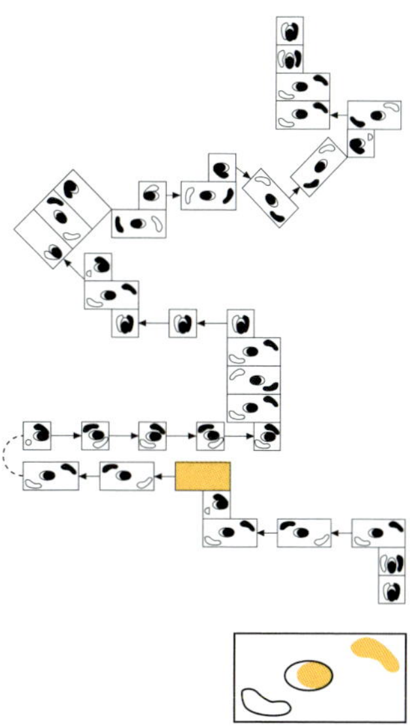

Posture 27 (left part): Bring all of the weight to the left foot, performing gong bu toward the east. Pass your left hand in front of the body as if you were cleaning off your knee while simultaneously extending your right arm to strike.

Breathing: Finish the exhalation.

Essence of the technique: Use the jijing force to strike at the vital point.

Posture 28 (right part): Bring your weight to the right foot and lift the left foot while rotating to the northeast. Stop with the right hand at the same time, passing it in front of the face.

Breathing: Inhaling.

Posture 29 (right part): Bring your weight to the left foot while the left hand continues the movement. Place your left hand at eye level, while the right hand stays in front of the body with the palm facing down.

Breathing: Continue inhaling.

Posture 30 (right part): Move the right foot forward, performing the ting bu position, and supporting it with the point on the floor. The arms will be the same as in the previous position.

Breathing: Finish inhaling.

Posture 31 (right part): Move the right foot forward, performing gong bu toward the east and passing the right hand in front of the body, as if cleaning off the knee. At the same time, strike forward with your left arm.

Breathing: Finish exhaling.

Essence of the technique: Use the jijing force, or the force of concentration, to strike the throat.

Posture 32 (left part): Bring the weight onto the left foot while lifting the right foot and rotating the body to the southeast. At the same time, stop with the left hand, passing it in front of the face.

Breathing: Begin inhaling.

Posture 33 (left part): Bring all of the weight onto the right foot while the right hand continues the movement and is placed at eye level. Your left hand is in front of the body with the palm facing down.

Breathing: Continue inhaling.

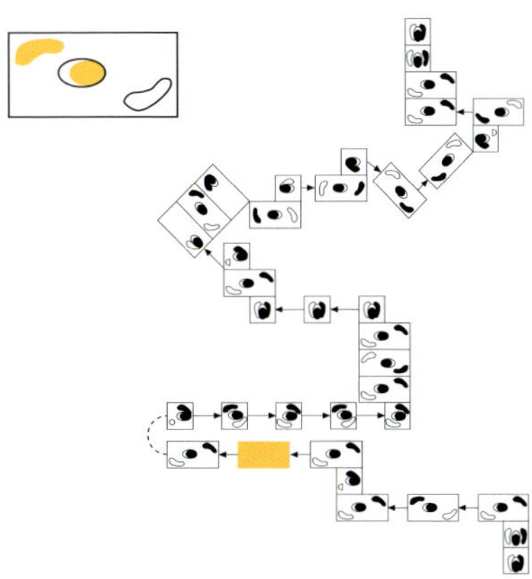

Posture 34 (left part): Move the left foot toward the east, performing the ting bu position and supporting the point on the floor. The arms are the same as in the previous position.

Breathing: Finish inhaling.

Posture 35 (right part): Look toward the southeast while lifting the right hand to eye level. The left hand is situated in front of the abdomen, parallel to the floor.

Breathing: Finish inhaling.

Essence of the technique: Use the luijing force, as if to divert a fist attack with your hands, without interrupting the direction.

Posture 36 (right part): Move the left foot toward the east, moving the point forward and supporting the heel down. Now move the right hand close to the face, pushing forward.

Breathing: Begin exhaling.

Posture 37 (left part): Move the weight to the left foot, performing gong bu to the east. Pass the left hand in front of the body, as if cleaning off the knee. At the same time, the right hand strikes forward.

Breathing: Finish exhaling.

Essence of the technique: Use jijing force to strike a vital point.

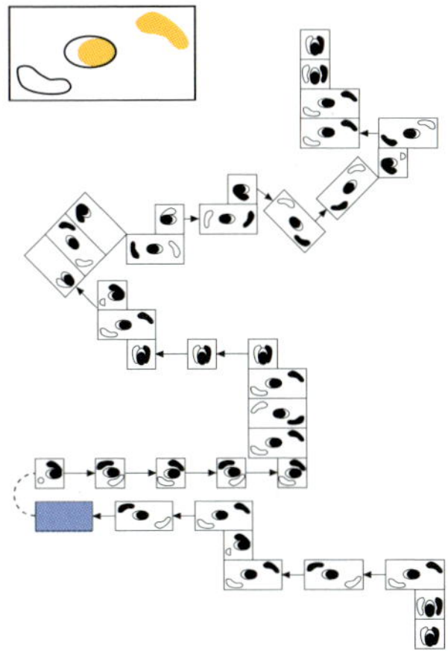

MOVEMENT 5

Chinese name: *Shou hui pi ba* (Strum the Lute), postures 38 to 40.

Posture 38: Move the right foot forward, performing an empty step and supporting the point on the floor. Lift the arms, beginning an inward rotation.

Breathing: Inhaling.

Posture 39: Support the sole of the right foot and, at the same time, lift the left one. Rotate the heel toward the east, performing the ting bu position. Place the arms as if they were holding a lute.

Breathing: Finish inhaling.

Posture 40: Continue the movement, supporting the heel of the left foot on the ground. Close your arms at the same time, keeping the hands with the palms facing inward, as if playing a lute.

Breathing: Exhaling.

Essence of the movement: Use jijing force to press, concentrating on three points: the center of the two palms and the center of the left foot.

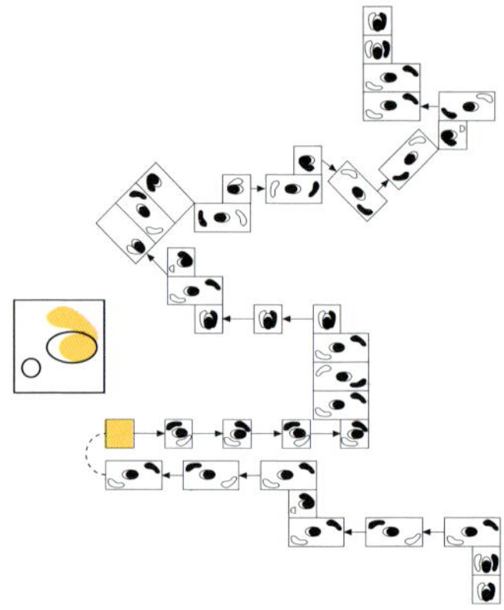

MOVEMENT 6

Chinese name: *Zou you dao juan hong* (Retreat and Rotate the Arms to the Right and Left), postures 41 to 53.

Posture 42: Move the weight onto the right foot, which is situated behind. Open the arms and look toward the southeast.

Breathing: Continue inhaling.

Posture 41: Bring all the weight to the right foot. Move the right hand backward at the same time, rotating the bust to the southeast and looking at the hand.

Breathing: Begin inhaling.

Posture 43: Lift the left foot and take a step back. Move the right hand, from the hip to eye level, drawing an arc to the southeast. At the same time, extend the left hand to the front.

Breathing: Finish inhaling.

Posture 44: Retreat the left foot, supporting the point of the foot and then the heel, with the point facing the northeast. Keep the feet at a distance equal to shoulder width from each other. Push the right hand forward and bring the left to the side.

Breathing: Exhaling.

Essence of the technique: Use the liejing force of division with the palm of the right hand toward the face. At the same time, push the air with your left hand.

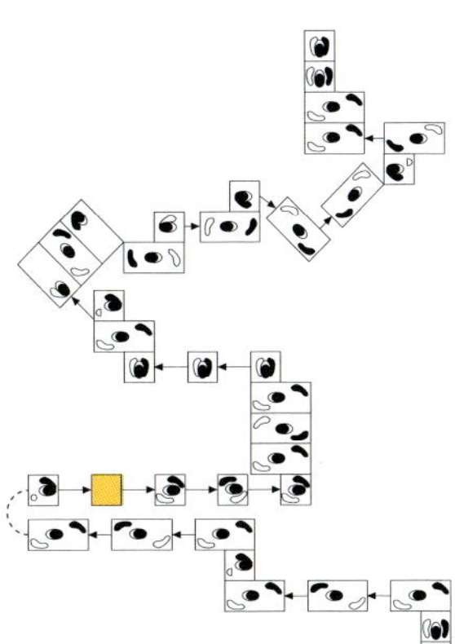

Posture 46: Move your left hand from the hip to eye level, drawing an arc to the northeast. Extend the right hand forward and lift the right foot while taking a step backward.

Breathing: Finish inhaling.

Posture 45: Bring your weight to the left foot and lift the left arm at the same time, rotating your chest to the northeast and facing the left hand to the northeast.

Breathing: Inhaling.

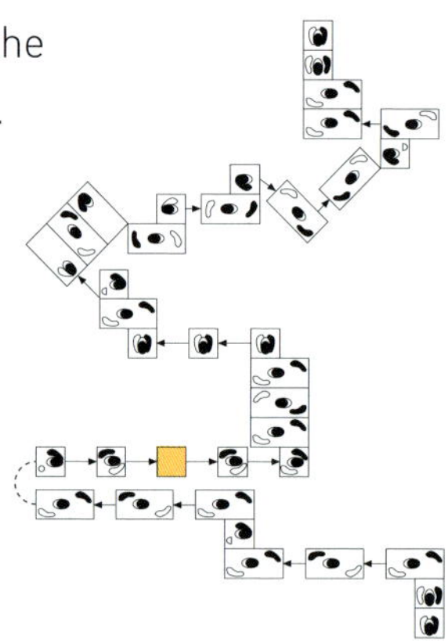

Posture 47: Retreat with the right foot, supporting the point and then the heel, similar to posture 44 but with the point of the foot facing southeast.

Breathing: Exhaling.

Posture 48: Move your weight onto the right foot, open your arms and look to the southeast.

Breathing: Continue inhaling.

Posture 49: Lift the left foot and take a step back. Move the right hand from the hip to eye level, drawing an arc to the southeast up. At the same time, extend the left hand forward.

Breathing: Finish inhaling.

Posture 50: Retreat with the left foot, supporting the point on the ground facing the northeast. Keep your feet at a shoulder-width distance from each other. Push the right hand forward and bring the left to the side, as in posture 44.

Breathing: Exhaling.

Essence of the technique: Use the liejing force moving your left and your right hand in opposite directions.

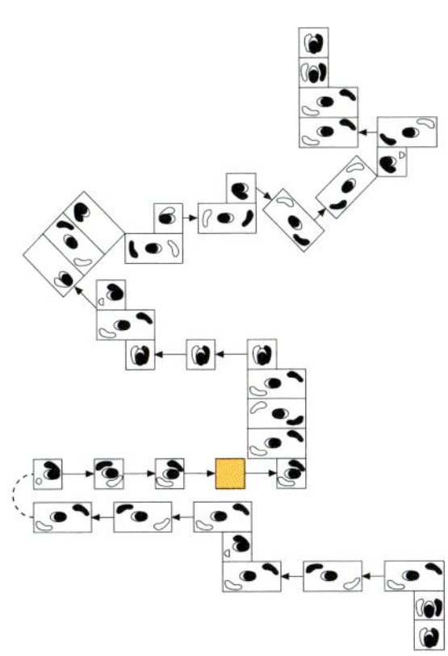

Posture 51: Bring the weight to the left foot. At the same time, lift the left arm, rotating the bust to the northeast and facing the left hand northeast.

Breathing: Inhaling.

Posture 52: Move the left hand from the hip to eye level, drawing an arc to the northeast up. Extend the right hand forward and lift the right foot, taking a step back.

Breathing: Finish inhaling.

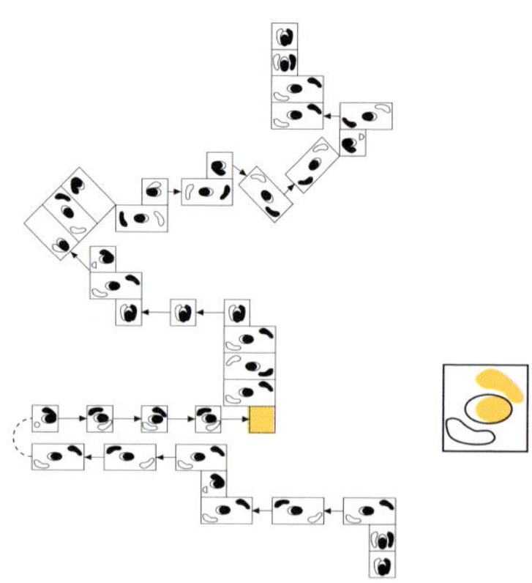

Posture 53: Retreat with the right foot, supporting the point and then the heel, as in posture 44, but facing the point of the foot to the southeast.

Breathing: Exhaling.

Third Section

MOVEMENT 7

Chinese name: *Zuo lan que wei* (Grasp the Bird's Tail to the Left), postures 54 to 66.

Posture 54: Lift the right hand to the southeast and, at the same time, bring the left hand forward, beginning a rotation downward. Bring the weight to the right leg.

Breathing: Begin inhaling.

Posture 55: Move the left foot back, bringing the arms together at the bust.

Breathing: Continue inhaling.

Posture 56: Lift the left foot and, bringing it back, perform the ting bu posture with the left foot and then support the point. At the same time, bring the left hand below the right, as if you were holding a ball.

Breathing: Finish inhaling.

Posture 57: With the weight on the right foot, move the left foot toward the east, supporting the heel. Lift the left arm up, while the right hand caresses the bird's tail downward.

Breathing: Exhaling.

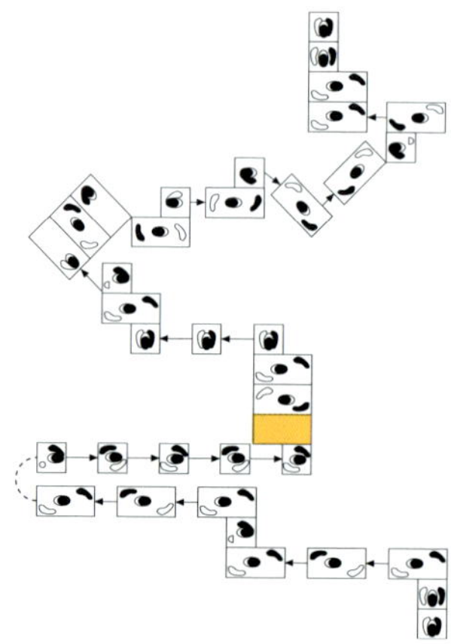

Posture 58: Support your left foot on the ground, performing gong bu with the right foot back, which presses down. With hands in front of the chest, keep the right four fingers below the forearm as if you were holding your left arm.

Breathing: Finish exhaling.

Essence of the technique: Use jijing for leverage.

Posture 59: Turning a little to the northeast, move the hands to the front without separating them. Draw a circumference toward the northeast and, turning the palms at the same time, lower them to the southeast. Lower the arms down, as if pulling. Arrive to the side and perform the complete movement while focusing your gaze. Move the weight from the left leg to the right leg.

Breathing: Inhaling.
Essence of the technique: Use the lujing force.

Posture 60: Continue the movement of the right arm upward, drawing an arc up to eye level. Hold your left forearm, with the palm facing down, steady in front of the abdomen, and move your left hand as if you were caressing the tail of a bird. Look at the right hand.

Breathing: Finish inhaling.

Posture 61: Bring the palm of your right hand down toward your left wrist, as if you were going to push it. Bring the weight of the arms to the east.

Breathing: Exhaling.

Posture 62: Move your weight forward, perform gong bu, pushing with the hands to the east up to chest height. Push the left arm forward with the palm of the right hand.

Breathing: Finish exhaling.

Essence of the technique: Use the jijing force, concentrating on expelling chi.

Posture 63: Open the hands in front of the chest with the palms facing down and bring the weight back. Push your hands down.

Breathing: Inhaling.

Posture 64: Bring your weight to the right foot and push the hands down.

Breathing: Continue inhaling.

Posture 65: Push your hands toward the floor until you reach the height of the abdomen, with all your weight on the right foot. Look forward and try to direct the fingers to the east, not down.

Breathing: Finish inhaling.

Essence of the technique: Use the pushing force, anjing (see page 22), downward.

Posture 66: Continue the previous movement as if the hands were pushing forward with a low-rising pressure. Move the weight from the left foot and push with the palms facing forward and the fingers up.

Breathing: Exhaling.

Essence of the technique:
Use the jijing force, moving from below upward.

MOVEMENT 8

Chinese name: *You lan que wei* (Grasp the Bird's Tail to the Right), postures 67 to 80.

Posture 67: Turn to the southeast, changing the weight from the left foot to the right. Lift the point of the left foot and look at your hands, which follow the movement of the core and open like a fan in opposite directions.

Breathing: Inhaling.

Posture 68: Shift your weight to the right foot, looking southeast and opening your arms even further. Focus on the three coordinations of tai chi (see page 37).

Breathing: Continue inhaling.

Posture 69: Once you achieve the greatest opening, close the arms and bring the right hand down to the left hand until the right rests on the left. At the same time, change the weight to the left foot. Lift the right foot and shift your gaze to the southeast.

Breathing: Continue inhaling.

Posture 70: Shift the weight to the left foot, performing the ting bu position to the west. At the same time, place the palm of the right hand upward and the left hand facing downward, as if they were holding a ball.

Breathing: Finish inhaling.

Posture 71: With the weight on the left foot, move the right toward the west, supporting the heel. Lift the right forearm up while pushing the left hand down in a caressing motion.

Breathing: Begin exhaling.

Posture 72: Support the right foot, performing gong bu with the back foot, which presses down. Your hands are in front of the chest, with the left four fingers below the right forearm, as if holding the arm.

Breathing: Finish exhaling.

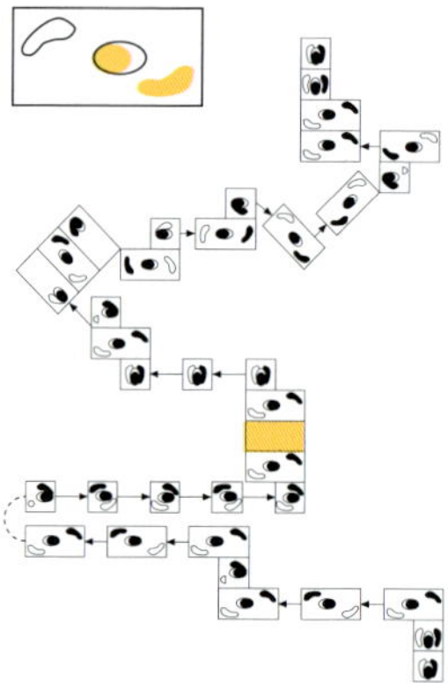

Posture 73: Turning northeast, push the hands to the front without altering the distance separating them. Make a circle with the hands toward the northeast and turn the hands at the same time, descending to the southeast. Lower the arms down, as if they were pushing. Bring them to the side and follow the motion with your eyes. To finish, switch the weight from your left foot to your right.

Breathing: Inhaling.
Essence of the technique: Use lujing force.

Posture 74: Continue moving your left arm upward, drawing an arc up to eye level. Pass your right forearm, with the palm facing down, in front of the abdomen. Look at the left hand.

Breathing: Finish inhaling.

Posture 75: Bring the palm of the left hand down to push the wrist of the right hand and move the weight backward with the arms toward the west.

Breathing: Exhaling.

Posture 76: Bring your weight forward, performing gong bu and pushing your hands to the west at chest height. The left palm pushes the right hand forward.

Breathing: Finish exhaling.

Essence of the technique: Use the jijing force to concentrate on expelling chi.

Posture 77: Open the hands in front of the chest with the palms facing down and bring the weight back. Lower the hands.

Breathing: Inhaling.

Posture 78: Now bring your weight back on the left leg and lower the hands.

Breathing: Continue inhaling.

Posture 79: Lower the hands to abdomen height, with all of the weight back, over the left foot. Look forward, with the fingers to the west, not down.

Breathing: Finish inhaling.

Essence of the technique: Use the pushing force, anjing, downward.

Posture 80: The hands, with the palms facing forward and the fingers up, rise up and move forward using the pressure from below. Bring the weight forward, onto the right foot.

Breathing: Exhaling.

Essence of the technique: Use the jijing force and push from above downward.

Fourth Section

MOVEMENT 9

Chinese name: *Dan bian* (Single Whip), postures 81 to 86.

Posture 81: Bring the weight back to the left leg and, at the same time, turn to the southeast, lifting the point of the right foot and then shifting your weight to your heel. Pass your left hand in front of your face with the palm facing you, then move the hand down and lower the right hand.

Breathing: Inhaling.

Posture 82: Pass your left hand in front of your face with the palm facing the south while the right hand passes your abdomen with the palm facing east. Follow the left hand with your eyes, and, at the same time, shift your weight forward and onto the left leg.

Breathing: Continue inhaling.

Posture 83: Bring your weight back and onto the right leg, continuing the rotation of the hands. Lower the left hand to the southeast and raise the right hand, palm inward, past your face. Direct your gaze to the right hand while bringing your weight forward.

Breathing: Finish inhaling.

Posture 84: Bring your weight to the right and the right hand to the southeast. At the end of the rotation, close the right hand, bringing the fingers together and forming a cluster (hooked hand). The left hand rises from below to face height. Direct your gaze to the right hand. With all of your weight on the right foot, the left foot moves to the left to perform the ting bu position.

Breathing: Exhaling.

Posture 85: Turn your chest and point the left foot to the east, supporting it on the heel. Look at the palm of the left hand, which moves from the southeast to the east, passing in front of the body.

Breathing: Inhaling.

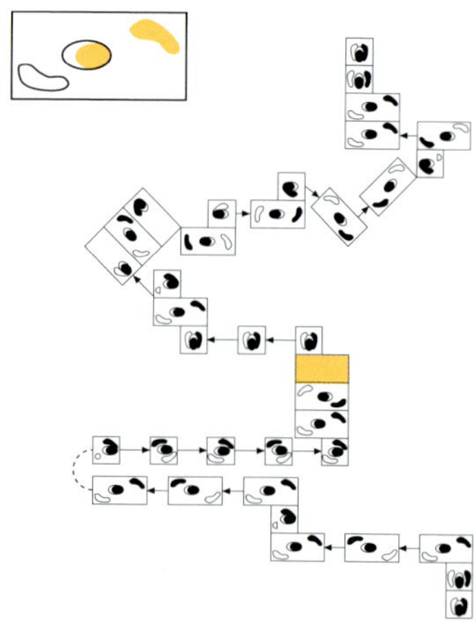

Posture 86: Support the left foot forward and perform gong bu toward the east. At the same time, shift your weight to the outside of the left foot and then push forward.

Breathing: Exhaling.

Essence of the technique: Use the pengjing force to expand.

MOVEMENT 10

Chinese name: *Yun shou* (Cloud Hands), postures 87 to 101.

Posture 87: Move the weight back and onto the right foot. At the same time, lift the point of the left foot, turning on its heel to point to the southeast. Follow the movement of the torso with your vision and look at the right hand in the direction of the southeast.

Breathing: Inhaling.

Posture 88: Open the right hand and begin a downward rotation. Bring the left hand up while keeping your weight forward on the right foot.

Breathing: Finish inhaling.

Posture 89: Shift your weight to the left foot, performing the *ma bu* posture (see page 33). Move the left hand toward the east in front of your face, with the palm facing inward, while the right hand lowers to the height of the abdomen, facing south with the palm facing down.

Breathing: Exhaling.

Posture 90: Continue the rotation of the hands, making two circles. After raising the left hand, switch your weight to your left foot and move the right toward it, supporting it on the point and then on the heel. Focus your gaze to the southeast.

Breathing: Inhaling.

Postures 91 and 92: Place your weight on the right foot and move your right hand in front of your face, palm facing inward, pointing to the southeast. Pass your left hand at abdomen level, also in the southeast direction, with the palm facing down.

Breathing: Exhaling.

Essence of the technique: Use the anjing force, but to the right instead of down.

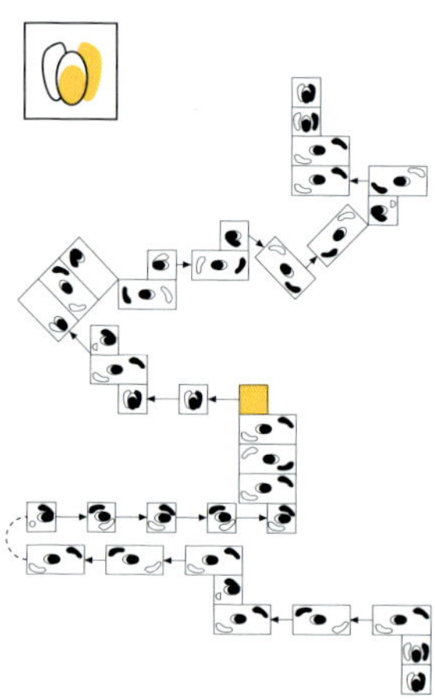

Posture 93: Lower the right hand and raise the left hand. Look at the right hand and bring the weight back, onto the right foot.

Breathing:
Begin inhaling.

Posture 94: Shift your weight forward to the left foot, performing the ma bu position. Pass the left hand in front of the face, with the palm facing inward, in the direction of the east, while the right hand lowers to the height of the abdomen in the direction of the south and with the palm facing down.

Breathing: Exhaling.
Essence of the technique: Use the anjing, or pushing force, not downward but to the right.

Posture 95: Continue the rotation of the arms, making two circles, first one and then the other. After lifting the left hand, move the weight to the left foot and move toward the right foot, supporting the point first and the heel after. Direct the gaze toward the southeast.

Breathing: Inhaling.

Postures 96 and 97: Move your weight to the right foot and pass the right hand in front of your face, with the palm facing inward, in the southeast direction. Pass the left hand at abdomen height, also toward the southeast, with the palm facing downward.

Breathing: Exhaling.

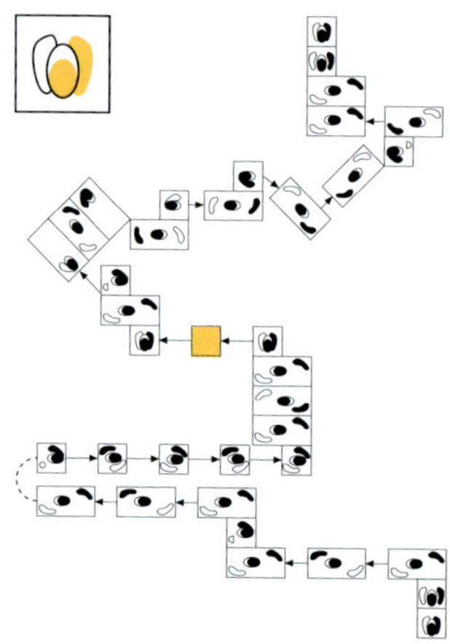

Posture 98: Begin with the right hand, which lowers while the left hand rises. Look at the right hand and move your weight onto the right leg.

Breathing: Inhaling.

Posture 99: Move your weight onto the left foot while performing the ma bu position. Pass the left hand in front of the face, with the palm facing inward, in the direction of the east. Meanwhile, the right hand passes at the level of the abdomen to the south with the palm facing downward.

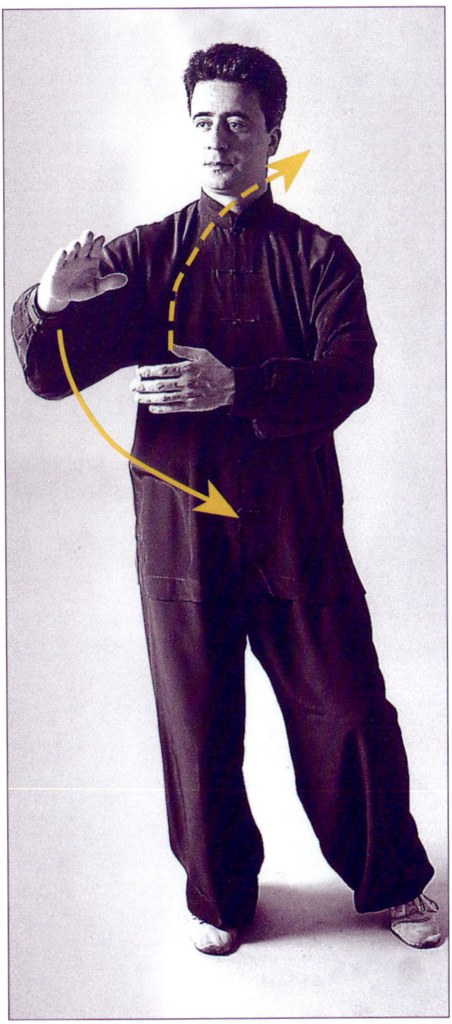

Posture 100: Continue the rotation of the arms, making two circles, first one and then the other. After raising the left hand, move your weight to the left foot and move the right foot close, supporting the point first and the heel after. Direct the gaze to the southeast.

Breathing: Inhaling.

Posture 101: Move the weight of the body to the right foot and pass the right hand in front of your face, palm facing inward, in the direction of the southeast. Pass the left hand in front of the abdomen, also in the direction of the southeast, with the palm facing down.

Breathing: Exhaling.

MOVEMENT 11

Chinese name: *Dan bian* (Single Whip), postures 102 to 106.

Posture 102: Move your weight onto the right foot and pass your right hand in front of your face, palm facing inward, to the southeast. Pass the left hand in front of your abdomen, palm facing down.

Breathing: Exhaling.

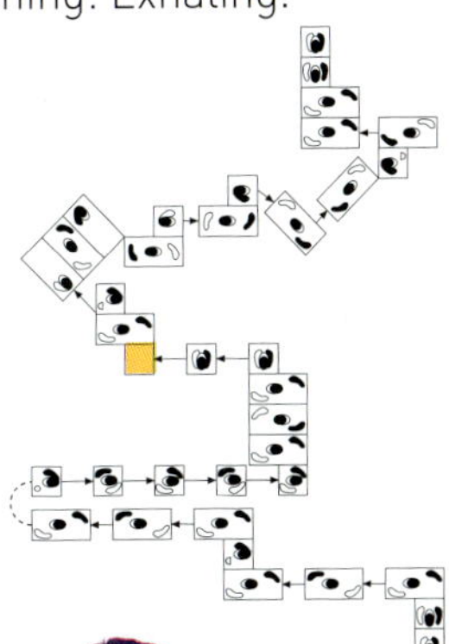

Posture 103: The right hand lowers and the left hand rises. Look at the right hand and move the weight to the right foot.

Breathing: Inhaling.

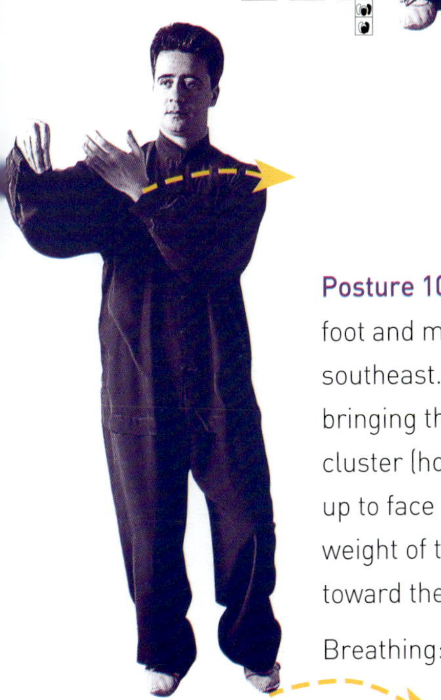

Posture 104: Move the weight of the body onto the right foot and move the arms, bringing the right hand to the southeast. Close the right hand at the end of the rotation, bringing the points of the fingers together and forming a cluster (hooked hand). The left hand passes from below up to face level. Direct the gaze to the right hand. Keep the weight of the body on the right foot, while the left moves toward the left to form the ting bu posture.

Breathing: Exhaling.

Posture 105: Turn the core and the left leg toward the east, supporting the heel. Look at the palm of the left hand, which moves from the southeast to the east, passing in front of your body.

Breathing: Inhaling.

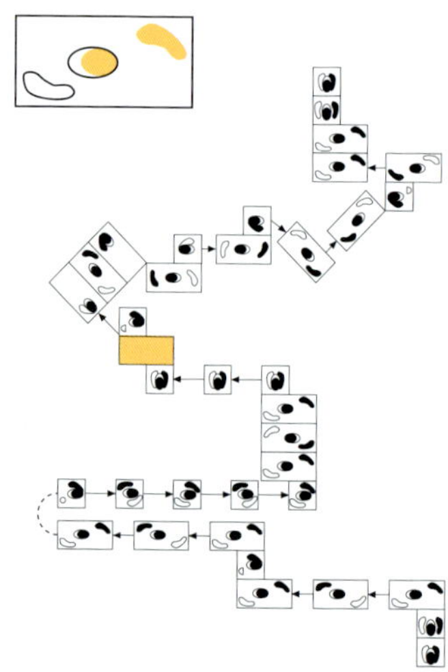

Posture 106: Support the sole of the left foot and perform gong bu toward the east, while simultaneously moving your weight onto it. Turn the palm of the left hand outward, then push forward.

Breathing: Exhaling.

Essence of the technique: Use the pengjing force to expand.

Fifth Section

MOVEMENT 12

Chinese name: *Gao tan ma* (High Pat on Horse), postures 107 and 108.

Posture 107: From the previous position, bring the weight to the left foot and perform the empty step, xu bu, moving the right foot forward toward the east and supporting the point of the foot. At the same time, open the right hand from the clustered position, making a turn counterclockwise, with the left palm facing up.

Breathing: Inhaling.

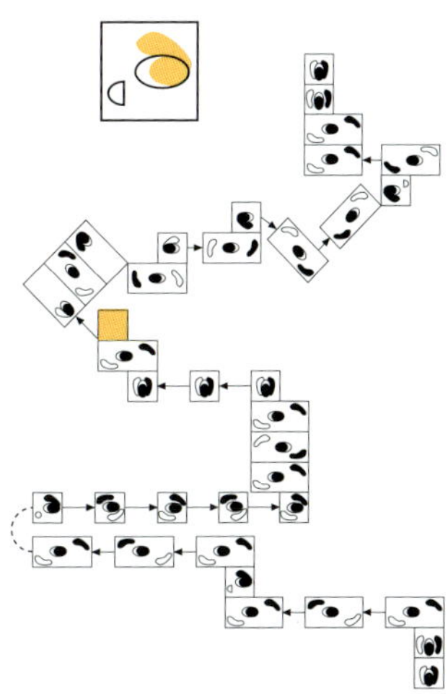

Posture 108: Perform the ting bu position with your weight on the right foot and the toes of your left foot touching the floor. Cross your hands as if stroking the mane of a horse, the left toward the west and the right toward the east.

Breathing: Exhaling.

Essence of the technique: Use the liejing force to divide.

MOVEMENT 13

Chinese name: *You deng jiao* (Right Heel Kick), postures 109 to 114.

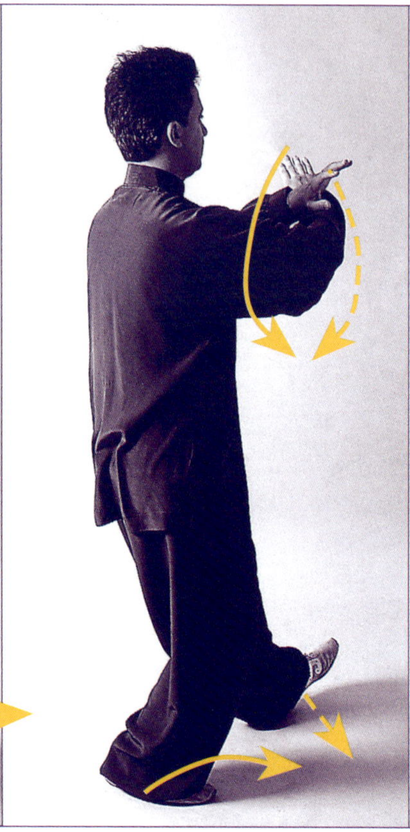

Posture 109: Bringing all your weight on the right foot, lift the left foot from the floor. At the same time, lift the left hand and cross it in front of your face with the palm facing inward. Lower the right hand with the palm facing east.

Breathing: Inhaling.

Posture 110: Lower the left hand to the northeast, supporting the heel. Turning the left hand toward the sternum, begin opening the hand toward the northeast.

Breathing: Continue inhaling.

Posture 111: Bring the weight forward to the left leg and lift the right foot to take a step forward. Open the hands, lowering them to bring them together in front of the abdomen.

Breathing: Continue inhaling.

Posture 112: Move the right foot toward the southeast, supporting the point while looking at it. Lift the hands up in front of the face with the forearms crossed, the right on the outside and the palms of both directed toward your face.

Breathing: Finish inhaling.

Posture 113: Bring the entire weight of the body back onto the left foot and lift the right knee with the point of the foot facing down. At the same times open the hands toward the southeast, like a fan.

Breathing: Exhaling.

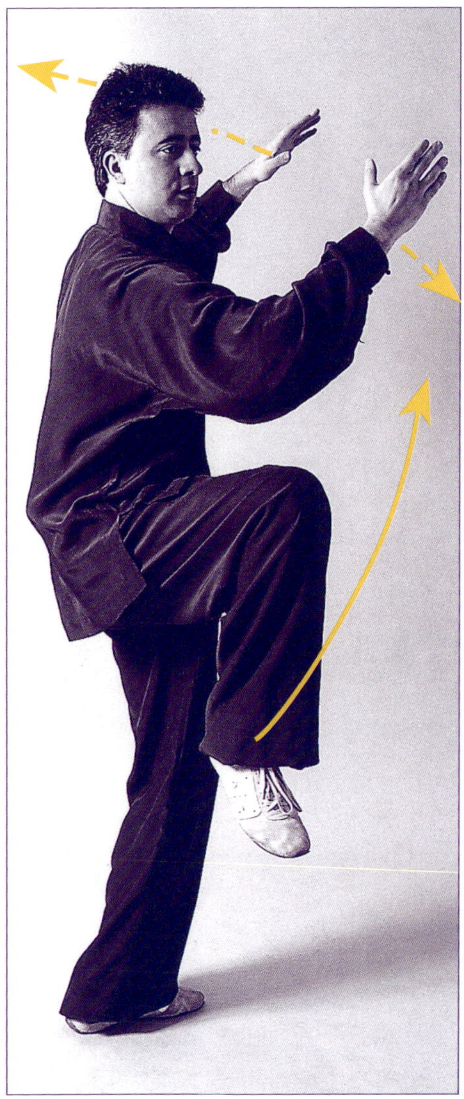

Posture 114: Extend the right leg and kick with the heel, bringing the foot up to shoulder height. The toes of the foot are pointed toward your face. At the same time, open the hands, respecting the three coordinations of tai chi. Have the right hand above the right leg and the left hand facing toward the northeast.

Breathing: Finish exhaling.

MOVEMENT 14

Chinese name: *Shuang feng guan er* (Attack the Ears with the Fists), postures 115 to 118.

Posture 115: Lower the right leg. Lower your hands with the palms facing up, while lifting the right knee and flexing the left foot.

Breathing: Inhaling.

Posture 116: Lower your hands until they're below the right knee. Keep your body upright.

Breathing:
Continue inhaling.

Posture 117: Lower the right leg in the direction of the southeast, supporting the heel at the same time. Begin the rotation of both arms upward and inward.

Breathing: Finish inhaling.

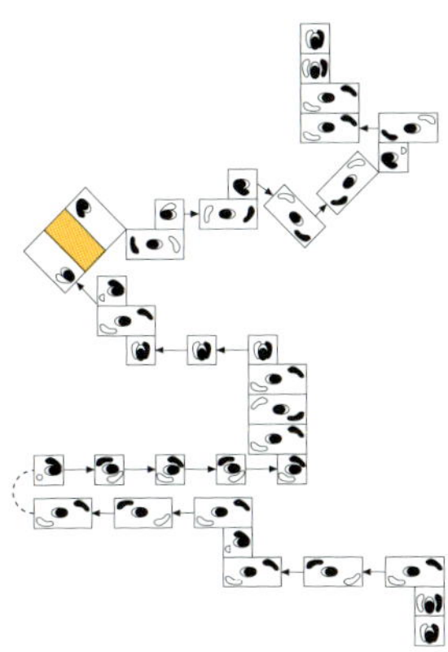

Posture 118: Bring the weight forward, performing gong bu and striking with the fist at head height. Keep a distance of eight inches between the fists.

Breathing: Exhaling.

MOVEMENT 15

Chinese name: *Zhuan shen zuo deng jiao* (Turn and Kick with Right Heel), postures 119 to 124.

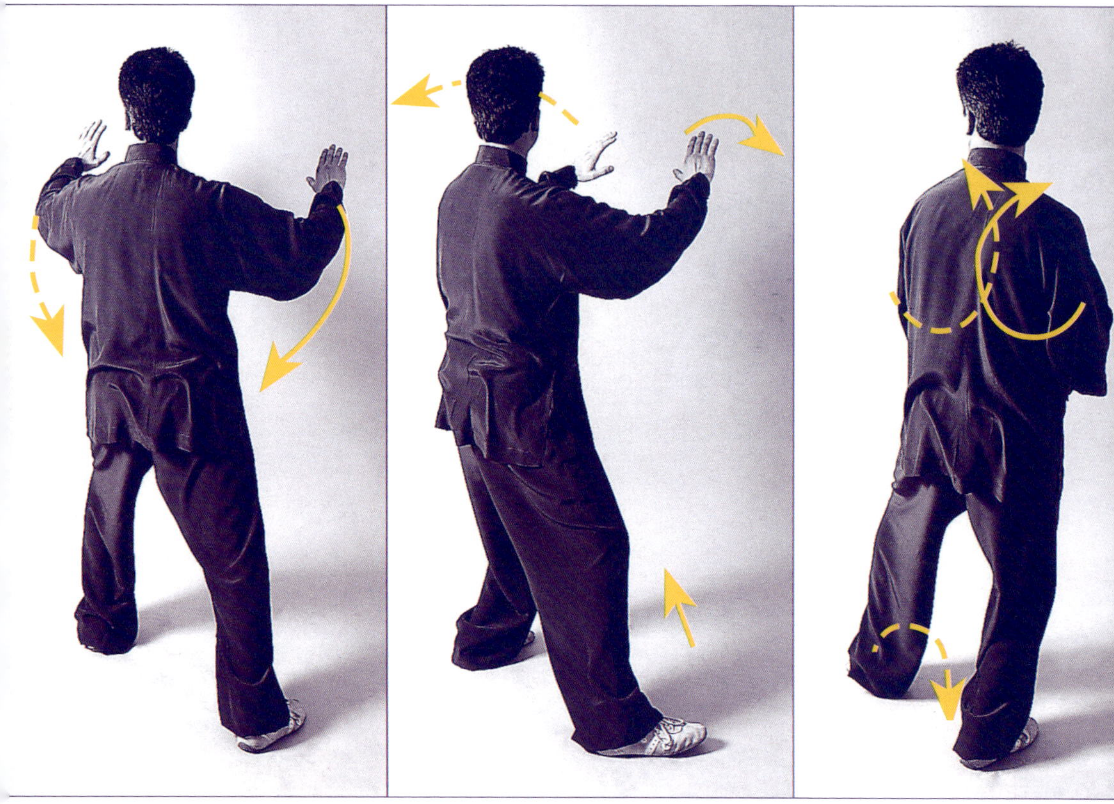

Posture 119: Bring the weight of the body onto the left foot and turn the chest 180° toward the northeast. At the same time, open your hands like a fan.

Breathing: Inhaling.

Posture 120: Bring the weight onto the left foot and follow with your torso, opening the hands.

Breathing: Continue inhaling.

Posture 121: Move the weight to the right foot and bring the left one back. Supporting your toes on the floor, hold your hands in front of the abdomen.

Breathing: Continue inhaling.

Posture 122: Continue the movement of the arms until they are in front of your face and the forearms are crossed, with the left on the outside. The palms of your hands are turned toward your face.

Breathing: Finish inhaling.

Posture 123: Lift your left knee with the point of the foot facing down. Begin opening the arms.

Breathing: Exhaling.

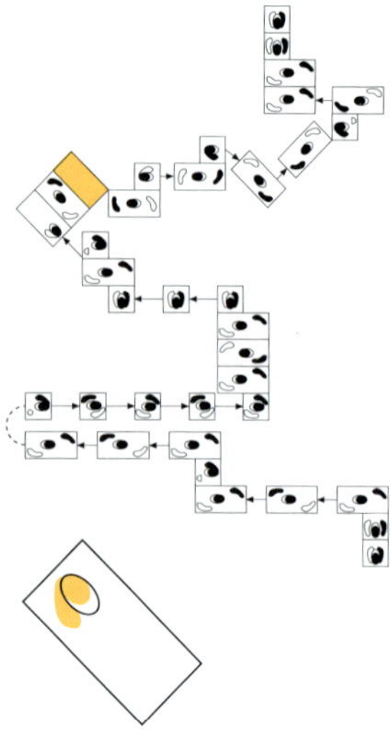

Posture 124: Extend your leg, kicking with the left heel and opening the arms, with the left arm stretched out over the left leg and the right arm pushing to the northeast.

Breathing: Finish exhaling.

Sixth Section

MOVEMENT 16

Chinese name: *Zuo xia shi du li* (Push Down and Stand on One Leg on Left Side), postures 125 to 131.

Posture 125: Lower the left leg and arm.

Breathing: Inhaling.

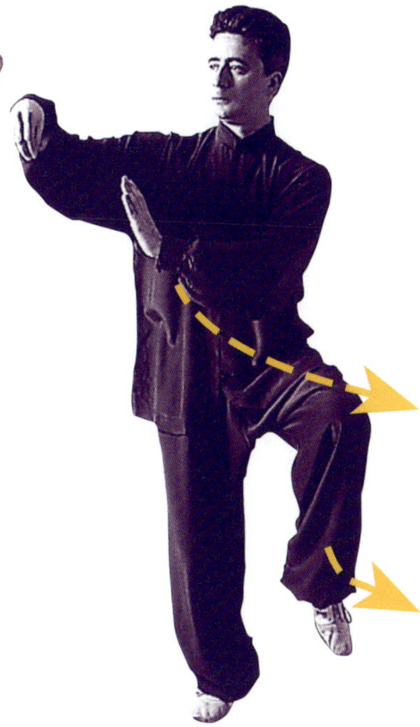

Posture 126: Balanced over the right leg, turn the core toward the northeast and extend the right arm, closing it into a cluster. Pass the right hand in front of your face and direct it down.

Breathing: Continue inhaling.

Posture 127: Lower the left leg toward the east, supporting first the heel with the point of the foot facing north. At the same time, bend the right leg. Look at your right hand toward the northeast.

Breathing: Continue inhaling.

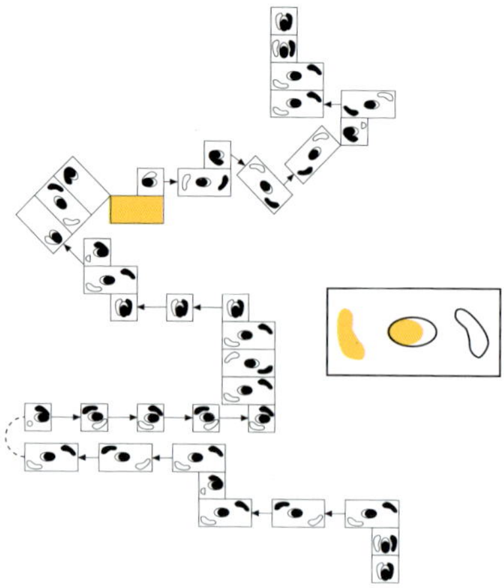

Posture 128: Descend in *pu bu* posture (see page 34) with the left leg extended and the right bent. Continue the rotation of the left hand, bringing it to the abdomen toward the west, close to the left foot. Have the right still closed in a cluster, directed toward the northeast. Look down and to the west. Keep the core and the head erect and the hips close to the ground.

Breathing: Exhaling.

Posture 129: Incorporating it, follow the circular movement upward until you arrive at gong bu. With your left hand in front of the knee, your hand faces north, the thumb open, as if it were holding an arm. Turn the right arm, with the fingers still closed and upward, close to your lower back.

Breathing: Finish inhaling.

Posture 130: Bring the weight forward and onto the left foot. Move forward with the right foot while you move the right arm up and the left arm down.

Breathing: Inhaling.

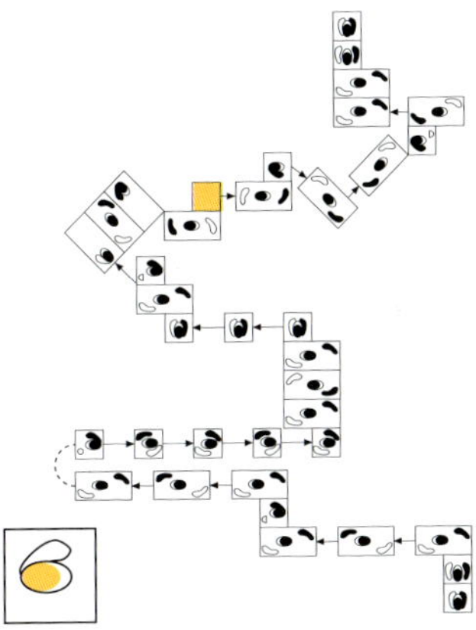

Posture 131: Lift your right knee, staying balanced on the left foot. Move the right hand upward until it reaches up to face height, with the palm concave and facing up as if holding an arm. Lower the left hand to the left side with the palm pushing toward the floor.

Breathing: Exhaling.

MOVEMENT 17

Chinese name: *You xia shi du li* (Push Down and Stand on One Leg on Right Side), postures 132 to 138.

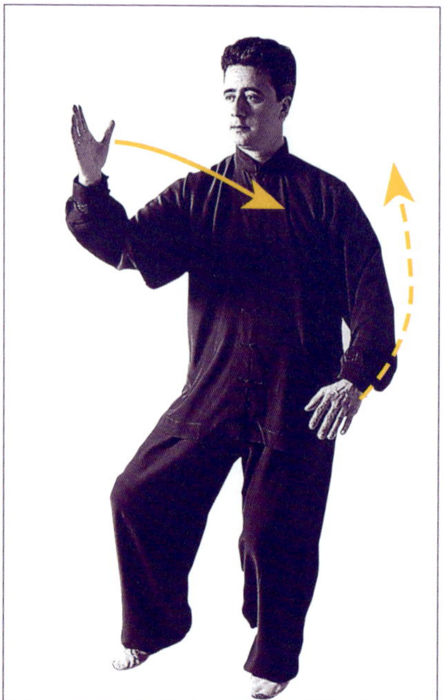

Posture 132: Lower the right leg, turning your core toward the southeast. Move your gaze toward the right hand in front of the face and raise the left hand.

Breathing: Inhaling.

Posture 133: Turn the head and the trunk toward the southeast. Keep the weight back on the left foot, with the point of the left foot supported on the floor. Lift the left hand up to face height with the fingers closed in a cluster. Bring the right hand toward the left side.

Breathing: Continue inhaling.

Posture 134: Move the right leg backward, supporting the heel and having the point of the foot facing south. Direct the gaze to the southeast, toward the left hand.

Breathing: Continue inhaling.

Posture 135: Lower down to the pu bu posture, with the right leg extended toward the west and the left bent. Have the right hand above the right foot and the left hand closed in a cluster toward the southeast.

Breathing: Finish inhaling.

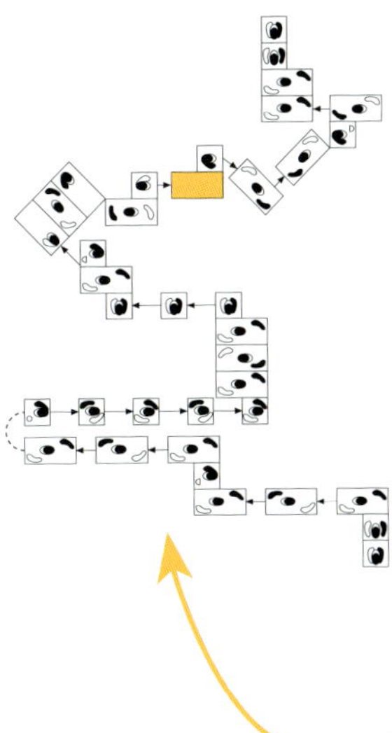

Posture 136: Rise in gong bu position, bringing the weight over the right foot. The right hand is in front of the face with the palm facing inward and to the south. The left hand is close to the left hip with fingers together and directed upward.

Breathing: Exhaling.

Posture 137: Move the weight toward the right foot and move the left foot forward. Lower the right hand and raise the left hand at the same time.

Breathing: Inhaling.

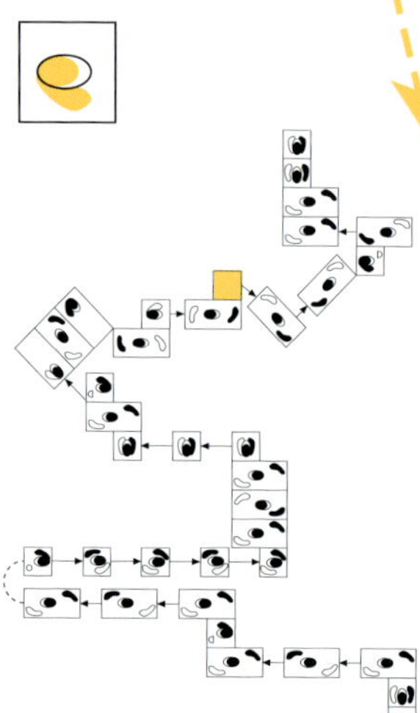

Posture 138: Lift the left knee, keeping the balance on the right foot. Bring the left hand upward until it is in front of your face with the palm facing up, as if supporting an arm. Lower the right hand to your right side at the same time, palm facing down.

Breathing: Exhaling.

Seventh Section

MOVEMENT 18

Chinese name: *Zuo you chuan suo* (Weaves with Shuttle), postures 139 to 149.

Posture 139: Turn the body southeast and lower the left foot with the point facing southeast. At the same time, lift the left hand and lower the right one, palms facing each other.

Breathing: Inhaling.

Posture 140: Lower the left foot and bring the weight toward it. Position the hands as if they were holding a ball. Look toward the southeast.

Breathing:
Continue inhaling.

Posture 141: Bring the weight onto the left foot and move it toward the right, performing ting bu. Point your right foot northeast and look in the same direction. Begin a rotation with the hands.

Breathing: Finish inhaling.

Posture 142: Move the right leg northeast, supporting the heel. Lift the right hand to the front with the palm facing in and push with the left hand from below upward.

Breathing: Begin exhaling.

Posture 143: Supporting the right foot, bring the weight forward. Continue the rotation with the arms.

Breathing:
Continue exhaling.

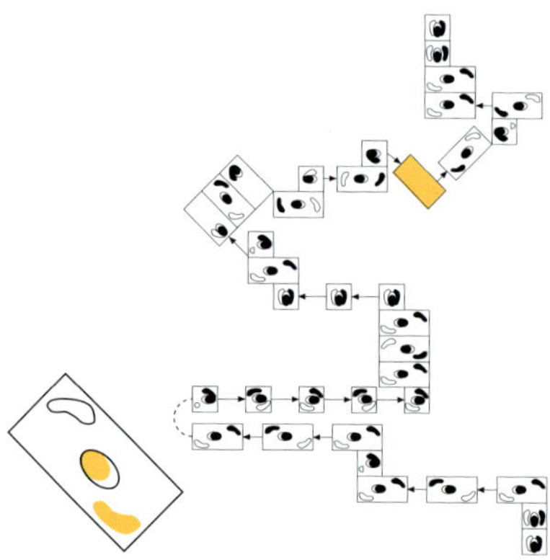

Posture 144: Bring the weight to the right foot, performing gong bu toward the northeast. Pass the right hand in front of your face with the palm directed outward. Push with the left hand in the same direction, extending the arm.

Breathing: Finish exhaling.

Posture 145: Bring your weight to the right foot and move the left foot forward. Turn the head southeast. Close the hands, palms facing each other.

Breathing: Inhaling.

Posture 146: Move the left foot forward, performing the ting bu position with the point of the foot facing southeast. Move the hands toward the northwest as if they were holding a ball.

Breathing: Finish inhaling.

Posture 147: Move your left leg southeast while supporting the heel. At the same time, lift the left arm and bring the right hand downward, pushing in the same direction.

Breathing: Exhaling.

Posture 148: Support the heel of the left foot forward and continue raising the left arm with the palm of the right hand facing in. Bring the right hand forward with the palm in the direction of the southeast.

Breathing: Continue exhaling.

Posture 149: Move the weight toward the left foot, performing gong bu. At the same time, lift the left arm in front of your face and push with the right hand forward.

Breathing: Finish exhaling.

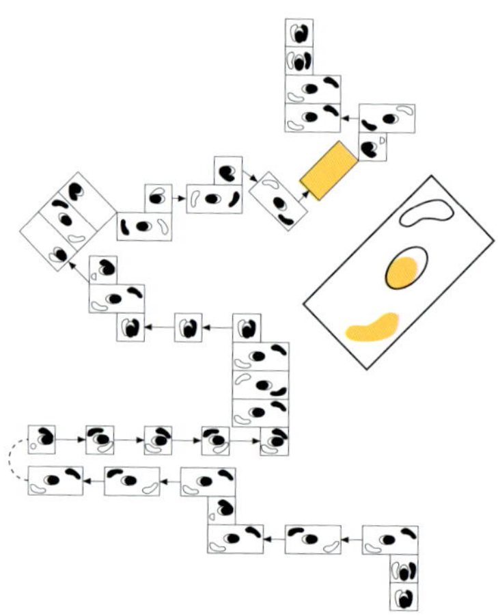

MOVEMENT 19

Chinese name: *Hai di zhen* (Pick Up the Needle from the Bottom of the Sea), postures 150 and 151.

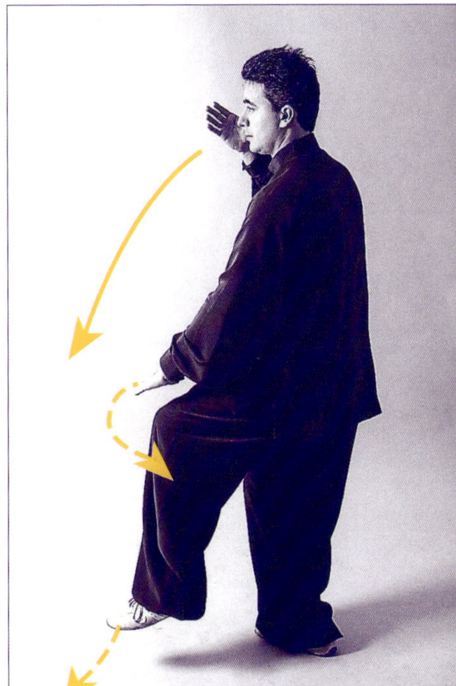

Posture 150: Bring the weight onto the left foot and turn the body toward the west, while the right leg moves forward to take an empty step, xu bu. Direct the gaze toward the northeast, following the movement first with the left hand and then with the right hand. Continue the rotation of the right hand, bringing it to the face with the palm facing inward, and look toward the west. Move the point of the left foot toward the west.

Breathing: Finish inhaling.

Posture 151: Lightly support the point of the left foot and, at the same time, lower yourself, bringing your weight back to the right leg. Lower the right hand, with the fingers pointing down and forward.

Breathing: Exhaling.

Essence of the technique: Use the wrenching force, caijing (see page 23), to lower down, as if the hand were tearing something down.

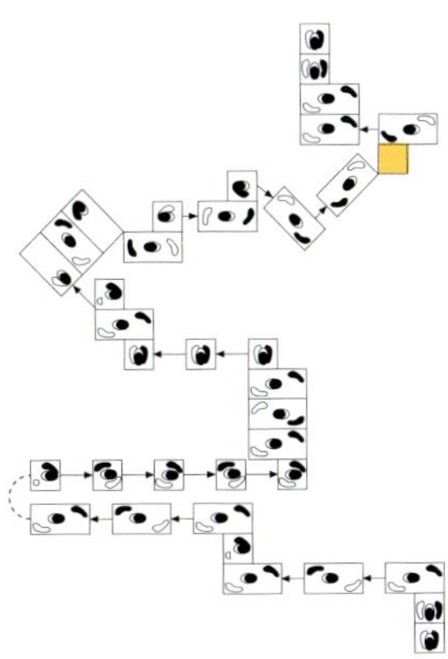

MOVEMENT 20

Chinese name: *Shan tong bei* (Fan Through the Back), postures 152 and 153.

Posture 152: Rise and bring your weight to the right foot. At the same time, lift your right arm and have the left hand close to the inside of the right forearm, with the palm directed toward your face.

Breathing: Inhaling.

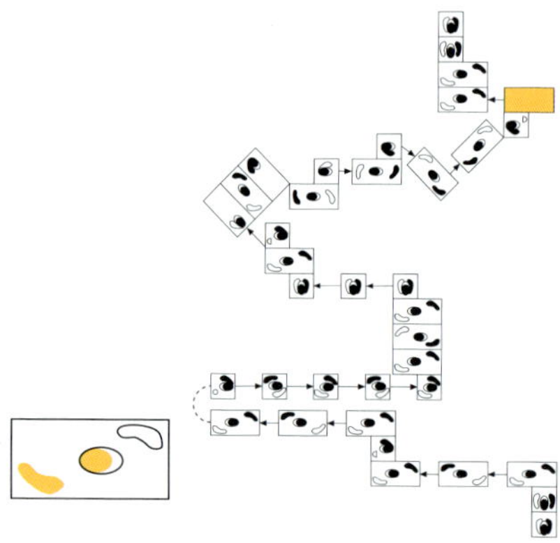

Posture 153: Move the left leg toward the west, performing gong bu. Maintain weight over the left foot, bringing your right arm over your head, the palm of the hand facing northeast. Position both the left and right palms toward the northeast.

Breathing: Exhaling.

Essence of the technique: Use the pengjing force, as if the arms opened into a fan.

Eighth Section

MOVEMENT 21

Chinese name: *Zhuan shen ban lan chui* (Turn Body, Block, Parry, and Punch), postures 154 to 160.

Posture 154: Move your weight to your right foot, turning the body 180° east. Bring your right arm toward the northeast, beginning a rotating movement from above going downward.

Breathing: Inhaling.

Posture 155: Move your weight to the left foot. Look toward the northeast. Bring your right arm in front of your core with the back of the fist facing up and your left arm above your head, palm facing north.

Breathing: Continue inhaling.

Posture 156: Bringing all your weight to the left foot, lift the right leg with the foot facing southwest. Turn your torso eastward and lower the left arm, passing it in front of the right while also lifting your right arm in front of the chest.

Breathing: Continue inhaling.

Posture 157: Lower yourself with the right leg forward. Move forward, lifting your left heel, and begin a horizontal rotation with the right forearm. Bring the left hand forward.

Breathing: Continue inhaling.

Posture 158: Bring all your weight to the right foot and lift the left. Move your right forearm with a rotation to the right side and stretch the left arm toward the east. Close the right hand.

Breathing: Finish inhaling.

Posture 159: Bring your left foot forward, supporting it on the heel. Strike toward the east with the right fist. Bring the left hand toward the body at the same time, palm facing south.

Breathing: Exhaling.

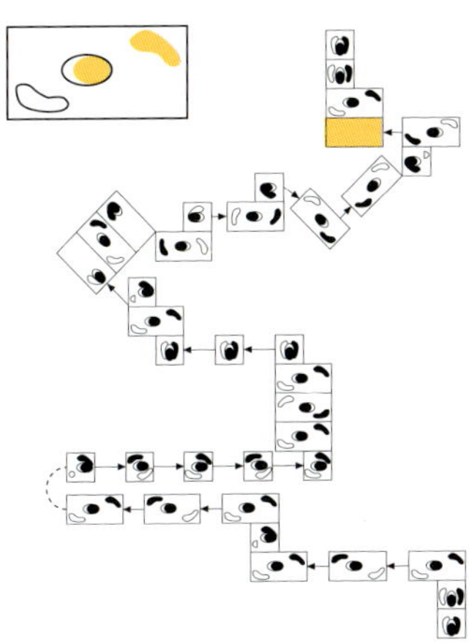

Posture 160: Move your weight forward, performing gong bu and simultaneously striking toward the east with your fist. Bring your left hand close to your right side with the palm facing the arm.

Breathing: Finish exhaling.

MOVEMENT 22

Chinese name: *Ru feng si bi* (Retreat and Seal), postures 161 to 164.

Posture 161: Shift your weight to the right foot while simultaneously sliding the left hand down to the right forearm. Open your right fist, palm facing up.

Breathing: Inhaling.

Posture 162: Open your arms outward.

Breathing: Continue inhaling.

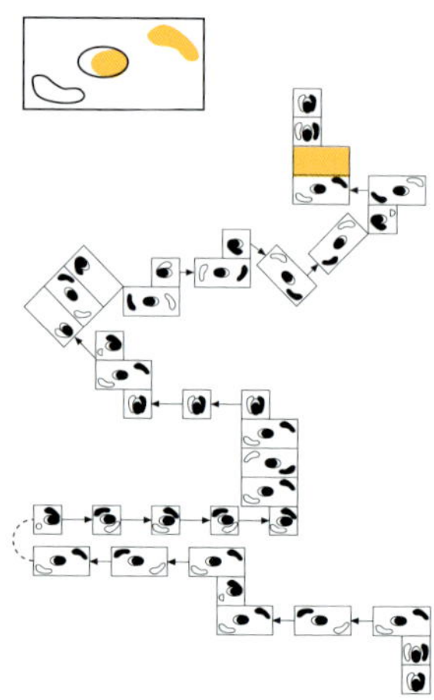

Posture 163: Move your weight to the right leg and lower yourself, hands close to your sides, with the left palm facing east.

Breathing: Exhaling.

Posture 164: Bring the weight to the left foot, performing gong bu toward the east while pushing the hands out.

Breathing: Finish exhaling.

MOVEMENT 23

Chinese name: *Shi zi shou* (Hands Crossed), postures 165 to 168.

Posture 165: Turn southeast, bringing the weight to the right foot while opening the arms.

Breathing: Inhaling.

Posture 166: Move the weight to the right foot, pointed toward the southwest. Continue opening the arms, maintaining the three coordinations of tai chi. Keep the palms facing south.

Breathing: Continue inhaling.

Posture 167: Shift your weight back to the left foot. Lower your hands toward the abdomen, palms facing up.

Breathing: Continue inhaling.

Posture 168: Bring the right leg close to the left leg and complete the position while upright, your legs shoulder-width distance apart.

Breathing: Exhaling.

Essence of the technique: Use the pengjing force to stop the hands from moving from the crossed position.

MOVEMENT 24

Chinese name: *Shou shi* (Closing), postures 169 to 171.

Posture 169: Open the hands outward, stretching the arms to shoulder height, palms facing down.

Breathing: Inhaling.

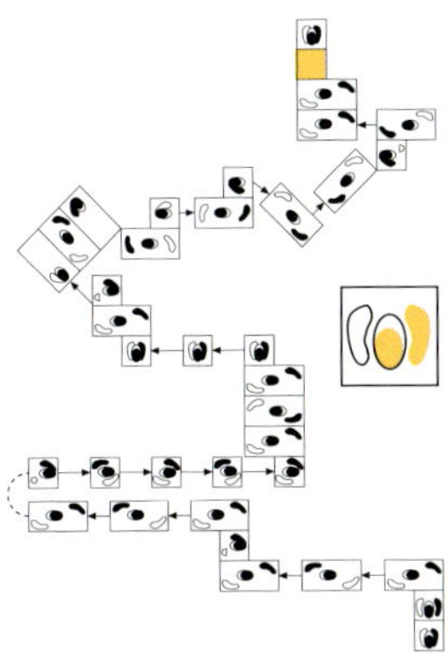

Posture 170: Move the hands close to the body and gently lower them to the height of tan tien. Bend your knees slightly.

Breathing: Begin exhaling.

Posture 171: Move the right foot toward the east and come to the starting position, feet together. Bring your hands to the sides, palms facing the body.

Taoist references: Return to the wu chi state.

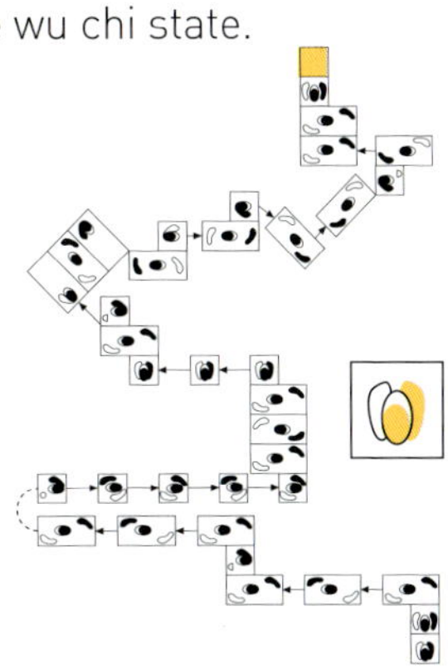

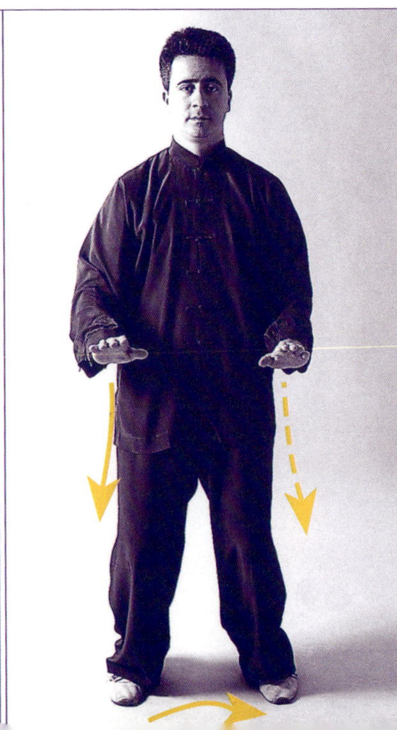

Glossary

bagua A Chinese martial art similar to tai chi, which emphasizes merging the mind and body to attain a higher level of consciousness.

chi The concept of an internal energy force governing all forms of life, central to the study of tai chi.

chi kung An ancient precursor of tai chi, in which chi is cultivated and directed through the body to improve health and increase vitality.

gong bu One of the fundamental stances of tai chi, typically used for attacking, in which the front foot is pointed straight ahead with the leg slightly bent, while the back foot is angled at 45°, resulting in a lunging position.

ming men An energy point located on the lower torso that, if manipulated correctly, can result in healing benefits.

tan tien The center of gravity in the standing body; it is located near the navel, by the *ming men*.

Taoism A religious and philosophical Chinese belief system that focuses on the notion of *tao* (harmony).

The Twenty-Four Movements An abridged version of tai chi, in which twenty-four postures are performed in a specific order. These forms are generally taught to beginners to give the student a general idea of tai chi.

xingyi An internal martial art, similar to bagua and tai chi, performed at normal speed and focused on the cultivation of chi.

yin and yang Part of the theory of both Taoism and tai chi, this concept proposes that every object has a necessary opposite in order to exist. It is further linked to the theory of universal interconnectivity, which argues that every object exists in relation to every other object, and nothing stands alone.

Further Reading

Books

Qiu, Pixiang, and Weimo Zhu. *Tai Chi Illustrated.* Champaign, IL: Human Kinetics, 2012.

Ting, William. *Essential Concepts of Tai Chi.* Bloomington, IN: Xlibris, 2015.

Zhuang, Henry Yinghao. *The Mind Inside Tai Chi Chuan: Sustaining a Joyful Heart.* Wolfeboro, NH: YMAA Publication Center, 2015.

Websites

American Tai Chi and Qiqong Association

www.americantaichi.org/about.asp

A national nonprofit organization designed to promote tai chi by offering resources for students as well as teachers.

Beginners Tai Chi

www.beginnerstaichi.com

A website catering to novices, explaining the fundamental concepts of tai chi.

Tai Chi for Health

www.americantaichi.net

An online journal focusing on the health benefits of tai chi.

Index

S

T

U / W

X

Y

Z